BUTTONS AND CORPSES

A Ghostly Fashionista Mystery

Gayle Leeson

Grace Abraham Publishing

D1059144

Gayle Leeson
Grace Abraham Publishing
A Division of Washington Cooper, Inc.
13335 Holbrook St.
Bristol, Virginia 24202

Publisher's Note: This is a work of fiction. Names, characters, places, and incidents are a product of the author's imagination. Locales and public names are sometimes used for atmospheric purposes. Any resemblance to actual people, living or dead, or to businesses, companies, events, institutions, or locales is completely coincidental.

Book Layout ©2017 BookDesignTemplates.com

Ordering Information:
Quantity sales. Special discounts are available on quantity purchases by corporations, associations, and others. For details, contact the "Special Sales Department" at the address above.

Buttons and Blows/ Gayle Leeson -- 1st ed.
ISBN 978-1-7320195-9-1

Also by Gayle Leeson

Writing as Gayle Trent

For Tim, Lianna, and Nicholas

I don't design clothes. I design dreams.
−RALPH LAUREN

Chapter One

Shimmying around the reception area of my fashion boutique, Designs on You, Max sang, "Trouble, trouble, I've had it all my days…"

While her great-aunt danced and crooned, my assistant Zoe played an imaginary saxophone, complete with mwah, mwah, mwah noises.

"Bessie Smith and Charlie Parker, you're not." I folded my arms. Watching my dainty gray and white tabby, Jasmine, frolic and bat at Max as she moved, I asked, "Et tu, Jazzy?"

"Oh, come on, darling," Max said. "We're only trying to lighten the mood. And we all have had trouble." She flattened a palm against her chest. "I'm dead, for goodness' sake."

"Yeah, and is your mom that much worse than mine? Really?" That said, Zoe put the make-believe sax back to her lips and began pressing the keys with both hands.

Shaking my head as the duo continued their song, I strode back into my atelier—or workroom, if you prefer—to finish a late 1930s-style dress that had a plunging tie-front bodice with shirring on the sleeves and a pleated skirt. The style had proven popular with the onset of summer, and I was replacing ready-to-wear sizes as they were bought in order to keep them in stock. It felt great to have to keep up with the demand for a product. I'd been in business just under a year, and I'd finally begun to build a reputation in this town.

And my parents had never been inside my shop.

Granted, they lived in Florida, and my shop was in Virginia, but still... They didn't even come home for Christmas this past year. We'd exchanged gifts and spent time together virtually. Even though Mom and I didn't have the closest relationship in the world, I'd missed her during the holidays and was bummed that I didn't get to be with her.

Max and Zoe were singing me the blues because I'd learned this morning that my parents were coming for a visit. I was thrilled to be seeing my dad. He was wonderful—a lot like his dad—known as Grand-pa Dave to me. But I was afraid my shop wouldn't live up to their—well, her—expectations.

I heard the door to the reception area open and then two unfamiliar voices, one male and one female, greeting Zoe. They couldn't see Max, of course.

"Hello, and welcome to Designs on You," Zoe said. "How may I help you this beautiful Saturday?"

Smiling to myself, I reflected on how far Zoe had come in the few months she'd been working here. I stood and went to see if there was anything the customers needed me for. Sometimes there wasn't. Frequently. customers came in for something off-the-rack or to browse. But, often, they required a special design.

I strode from the atelier into the reception area. "Hi, there. I'm Amanda Tucker."

"Amanda, we've heard so much about you," the woman said, extending her hand.

Shaking her hand, I said, "I'm flattered to hear that." I shook the man's hand as well.

"I'm Selma Greenfield," the woman continued, "and this is my husband, Stuart. We'd like for you to make us costumes for the Renaissance Festival that's coming to Brea Ridge in August."

"Renaissance Festival?" Max asked. "What's a Renaissance Festival? It sounds like something I'd positively adore!"

I smiled and tried to ignore Max's enthusiasm. "I didn't realize there was going to be a Renaissance Festival in Brea Ridge this year. That's fantastic."

"Yes, well, Stu and I are over the Brea Ridge chapter of the Southern Appalachian Renaissance Society," Selma said.

"And we're honored to be hosting this year's festival," Stu added. "We certainly hope you young ladies will attend."

"Are you off your nut?" Max asked. "Of course, we'll be there!"

"Off your nut?" Zoe echoed. Eyes widening, she said, "Sorry—that's an expression my great-aunt uses to mean, like, are you kidding?" She gave a little laugh. "You bet I plan on coming to the festival. I've never been to a Renaissance Faire."

"Oh, you'll love it," Selma said, stepping closer to Zoe. "With your blue hair, you should come as a fairy."

"I'm not much into tutus and gossamer wings." Zoe frowned slightly before bending to pick up Jazzy. "What else have you got?"

"You can be anything you'd like." Stuart took some business cards from his pocket and handed one to Zoe and one to me. "That's the fun of it. Now, on to why we're here in your fine establishment, Ms. Tucker. Selma and I would like to be Macbeth and Lady Macbeth this year."

"That's right." Selma turned to me. "We've never been the Scottish king and his wife before, and I feel it'll be great fun."

"Let me get a notepad." I moved to the desk and took out a steno pad. "At what point in the play would you like your characters to represent? As I'm sure you're well aware, the costumes in the play change with the mood of the play."

"Huzzah!" Stuart jabbed a fist into the air.

Max gasped. "Amanda is most certainly not a hussy, you overgrown dewdropper!"

Zoe barely stifled a giggle.

Now looming over Stuart, Max insisted, "You take that back! Take it back right now!"

"You know the play!" Stuart continued, unaware of the drama he'd caused.

"Huzzah," I said. "That's a variation on hurrah, right?" I knew what the word was, but I needed for Max to stop distracting me, and there was no way she would if she thought Stuart Greenfield had insulted me.

Stuart gave a little shudder. "Sorry—I just got a chill. Anyway, yes, dear. Huzzah is an exclamation we often use to show enjoyment." He gestured to the clothes I had on display. "I'm simply delighted we came to the right place. Not only do you obviously know fashion design, but you are familiar with Macbeth."

"Yes, well. As I said, I'll need to know whether you want your characters to appear as they would in the beginning, middle, or end of the play." I jotted the Greenfields' names at the top of the page. "And would you like the costumes to be early Gothic in style, or do you prefer Elizabethan?"

"I'd like the costumes to feel as authentic as possible," Selma said. "And let's go dark and a little bit creepy. What do you think, Stu?"

"Oh, I agree absolutely...so long as we don't frighten any children who'll be in attendance," he said.

"Okay. So early Gothic it is." I wrote down the time period and that the couple wanted their costumes to be creepy without being scary. "With Macbeth being Scottish, what color tartan would you want incorporated into your costumes—if any?"

"Tartan." Stuart nodded. "That's a wonderful idea. I have no idea what colors though. Do you, Sel?"

His wife shook her head. "No idea. I'd never given it any thought before."

I picked the tablet up off the desk. The tablet had once belonged to me, but I'd given it to Max so she could read, stream shows, and video chat. For a ghost, Max was awfully handy with technology. But since I'd never replaced the tablet, I still used it on occasion.

Opening a search engine, I typed in Macbeth tartan and instantly found the colors. I turned the tablet toward the Greenfields. "As you can see, the Macbeth tartan has a modern version and an ancient version—both of which utilize blue, red, green, black, yellow, and white. Since you're aiming for authenticity, I'll use the ancient form and will incorporate it minimally."

"Yes, yes, that's fine." Stuart looked at Selma. "I'm looking forward to seeing what Ms. Tucker produces."

"Well, before we do any measurements or start on any garments, I'll do sketches of the costumes and either give you a call or text you a photo of what I have in mind to make sure we're on the same page," I said.

The Greenfields agreed that sounded good to them, gave me both their cell numbers, and left.

Zoe immediately asked Max, "What in the world is a dewdropper?"

"A man who doesn't have a job," she said. "I figured if he spent all his time playing dress-up, he was a dewdropper. Of course, I was angry at him for calling Amanda a hussy at the time."

"Aunt Max, you're the elephant's eyebrows," Zoe said with a grin as she placed Jazzy onto the floor.

"Ah, aren't you the berries?" Max winked. "I wish I could give you a hug. Both of you."

Jazzy flopped down and rolled over in front of Max.

"And you, you lovely girl, you know I'd hug you too." Max laughed. "So, can I read this play online?"

Later that afternoon, Zoe and I got the shop tidied, and then I coaxed Jazzy into her carrier. Max was lounging on the worktable in the atelier reading *Macbeth*.

"Goodbye, darlings!" she called. "Don't do anything I wouldn't do!"

"What *wouldn't* she do?" Zoe muttered to me.

"I heard that!" Her reprimand was countered by her peal of laughter.

"Are you in a rush to get home today?" I always picked Zoe up and took her back home on Saturdays.

"No, why?"

"I'd like to stop by the antique store and see if there's anything I might be able to use for the Macbeth costumes," I said. "If you need to get home, I'll go by there some other day."

"I don't. Plus, I've never been in there."

"Really? You might find something you'll like." I smiled, looking forward to seeing how the teenager would react to the some of the old-fashioned items inside the shop.

"We'll ask my friend, Cassie, of the Abingdon Gifting Co., to watch Jazzy while we browse at Cross's Antiques," I said.

"That's another shop I've wanted to go inside but haven't visited."

We were lucky enough to find a parking spot not terribly far from Cassie's shop. We got out, and Zoe waited on the sidewalk while I came around and took Jazzy's carrier from the backseat.

"You really are kinda like a Bond villain carrying that cat around almost everywhere you go," Zoe said.

"And have you ever seen a Bond movie?" I asked.

"No, but Bond villains are stereotypical—and they carry around their cats." She shrugged her bony shoulders. "At least, that's what I've heard."

I expected Cassie's shop to be busy on a Saturday afternoon, but I didn't expect the chaos that was happening when we went inside. I quickly got a handle on the situation, though, having been in a similar predicament myself.

"Quick! Close the door!" I shoved Jazzy's carrier toward Zoe, so I could help Cassie and Sarah Conrad corral Biscuit and Gravy, Joey Conrad's ferrets.

While Cassie and Sarah tried to catch Biscuit, the white ferret, who was playing keep away with a vanilla bath bomb, eight-year-old Joey and Cassie's mom stood near the front window laughing. The pair of them were obviously enjoying the show.

"Lisa, where's Gravy?" I asked.

"Honey, we don't sell gravy," she said. "But Cassie has some delicious jams over there."

"Gravy is the brown ferret," I said.

"Oh!" She looked around. "He was in the Brotique area a second ago."

I spotted Gravy running toward the back of the store with a tin of beard balm. At least, the hyperactive critters apparently wanted to smell nice.

Before I could take off after Gravy, Biscuit streaked past me with the bath bomb, ran up Joey's left leg, and hid in the backpack.

Lisa clasped her hands together. "Isn't that the cutest thing?"

Cassie shot her mother a look that clearly said *no*.

"Joey, get that bath bomb away from him," Sarah said.

"Aw, c'mon, Mom." He frowned up at her. "You're probably gonna have to pay for it anyway."

"Of course, I'm going to pay for it, but it might kill him if he eats it."

His mouth forming a tiny *o*, Joey took the backpack off his shoulders and tried to extricate the vanilla scented bath bomb from Biscuit's paws. "He doesn't want to give it up."

"I've heard ferrets like eggs," Cassie said. "I have a boiled egg in my mini fridge. I was planning on putting on my chef's salad at lunchtime, but I forgot."

"They both adore eggs," Sarah said. "Could I buy that egg from you? It might help us get Gravy too."

"You're welcome to it." Cassie quickly retrieved the egg, placed it on a small, decorative cutting board, and sliced it in half.

When Gravy saw Sarah trading Biscuit a treat for the bath bomb, he came running with the beard balm. It was charming to see how quickly he relinquished the beard balm for his half of the egg. After they'd eaten, Joey returned them to his backpack.

"We'd better go, Mom," he said.

"Yeah." Sarah gave us a wan smile. "Now that they've eaten, they'll need to...go...soon. I'll try to stop in one day next week, Cassie."

"Okay."

"Oh, let me pay you for—"

"It's on me," Cassie interrupted her. "Don't worry about it."

It was only after Sarah, Joey, and the ferrets left, that I realized Jazzy was softly growling.

"It's okay, Jazzy," I said.

Cassie rubbed her forehead. "Still want a ferret, Mom?"

Lisa laughed. "I'd love one. Although after seeing those two together, maybe I should get a pair."

"I'm just glad I had the forethought to hide the bath salts when I saw Sarah and Joey coming up the sidewalk," Cassie said. "I can't even imagine what a mess *that* would've been."

"We only stopped in to say hi," I said. "We'll come back by next week." I nudged Zoe out the door.

When we got out onto the sidewalk, I told Zoe, "I think Cassie has had all the excitement she can stand for the time being. We'll take Jazzy into the antique shop with us."

The instant we walked into Cross's Antiques, Jazzy resumed her growling. I looked around to see if Sarah and Joey had stopped in here. That wouldn't make sense, though—they'd seemed to be in a rush to get the ferrets home.

I shivered. "It's kinda chilly in here, don't you think?"

"I wouldn't say that." Zoe looked around the shop. "But I do feel a cold spot—like I do sometimes around Max. I think this place is haunted."

Chapter Two

Violet Cross greeted us with a warm smile. "Good afternoon!" She wore a lightweight white cardigan with her trademark brooch—a cluster of violets—below her left shoulder. "Are you ladies looking for anything in particular today?"

"Not really. We'd simply like to browse." I introduced Zoe to Ms. Cross.

"What a pleasure," Ms. Cross said. "Let me know if you have any questions about anything."

"I have a question," Zoe said. "Do you have any ghosts in this shop?"

Ms. Cross chuckled. "My dear, I imagine there are a number of ghosts in here—figurative ones, at the very least. You'll see what I mean when you wander the aisles."

"You know, my cloche hats sold well during the winter months," Zoe said, as we wandered down the first dusty row of knickknacks. "Do you think I could make some hats for this upcoming Renaissance Faire? Like wimples and stuff?"

"I think that's a great idea," I said. "Plus, I'm impressed you know what a wimple is."

"Well, we read a Shakespearean play in English every year." She shrugged. "I figure maybe you could help me find some patterns of things that wouldn't be too hard for me to make."

"Of course, I will." I made a mental note to find out what type of hats sold well at or for Renaissance festivals.

"Eww." Zoe stopped.

"What is it?" I followed the direction of her gaze to a glass-eyed doll sitting on a rocking horse.

The doll was saying, "Mama...Mama..."

"That's the creepiest thing I've ever seen," Zoe said. "Now I see what Ms. Cross meant about there being a bunch of ghosts in this place."

I grinned. "It's not *that* bad."

"Yeah, well, I'm getting away from it." She hurried over into another section of the shop.

Ms. Cross's shop was like a treasure hunt. Nothing was in any particular place, and I never knew what I might find. Today, the first thing I found was a set of brass tree-of-life buttons. I also ran across a card of a dozen metal grapevine buttons.

I was examining some enamel buttons when a needlepoint portrait caught my eye. It was of a toddler with wavy hair and brown eyes. The child wore a rose-colored top beneath an olive-hued pinafore or vest of some kind. The portrait was large.

Setting my buttons aside, I walked over and picked up the portrait. I marveled at all those tiny stitches. And yet this masterpiece that someone had so painstakingly created wound up here in an antique shop. Unwanted. The thought nearly brought me to tears.

"What are you doing?"

I started at the sound of Zoe's voice. "Look at this. Isn't it amazing?"

"Yeah. Wonder how many hours that took to make?"

"I have no idea, but I imagine it was a lot," I said. "Why did no one want this? I mean, can you imagine someone in your family making this beautiful portrait and then when—" I didn't want to say *when they died* although that's when I imagined the piece was brought here. "—when the time comes to go through his or her things, no one in the family wanted this?"

"It could be haunted."

"Zoe!"

"Look at those eyes." She shuddered. "See how they follow you? Or, at least, *one* of them is always following you."

"They are not." I lowered my voice. "And why are you suddenly freaked out by the thought of ghosts?"

"I'm not freaked out by *all* ghosts—only the ones I'm not related to."

"Well, I'm buying this portrait," I said.

"Why?"

"Because someone worked awfully hard on this piece, and I appreciate it. I'm buying it and cleaning it up because I admire the craftsmanship."

"You're insane. That thing is going to wind up haunting us all," she said. "Aunt Max is gonna hate it."

"Come with me." I walked back over to the table where I'd left the buttons I'd chosen. "Grab those for me, would you? I can't carry Jazzy, the portrait, and the buttons too."

"I've got your buttons," she said, as she trailed behind me.

"Did you find anything you liked?" I asked.

"No."

I thought maybe she was being reticent. "If you did, I'll get it for you—"

"I didn't." This time her voice was firmer. "I really need to get home."

"All right." I took my items to the register. There was a framed photograph of a man on the shelf behind the counter. It appeared to have been taken in the late 1800s. In all my visits to Ms. Cross's shop, I'd never noticed the photo before. "Is that new? Is he a relative?"

Ms. Cross smiled. "He isn't a relative, dear. Nor is the photo new. His name is Thomas Wortley. Isn't he handsome?"

"He certainly is," I said.

The man had light hair and eyes, was clean-shaven, and was wearing a suit with a bow tie.

I felt a waft of cold air and exchanged glances with Zoe.

"Maybe he's the one who haunts this place," Zoe said. "He looks nice enough in the photograph."

Laughing, Ms. Cross rang up my items and gave me a total as she put them in bags. I handed her my debit card.

"Come again, dears," she called as we left.

"We will," I said.

"Speak for yourself," Zoe muttered as we left the shop.

After dropping Zoe off at home, I went to Grandpa Dave's house. I'd called him on the way, and he'd asked if I wanted to make a pizza and watch a movie with him. I told him I'd love nothing more.

He was sitting on the front porch waiting for Jazzy and me when we pulled into the driveway. I opened the back door of the car and then opened the carrier, knowing the cat would run straight to Grandpa Dave. She adored him almost as much as I did. She was on his lap by the time I climbed up the stairs and took a seat on the swing.

"I take it Jason has a wedding tonight?" he asked.

I nodded as I set the swing in motion. "He's pretty much booked solid through the end of August." My boyfriend, Jason, was a photographer.

"That's good for him, but I imagine it's rough on a relationship."

"Not really. We still see each other during the week." I smiled. "When you're self-employed, week-ends are kind of irrelevant."

"Point taken."

"What about you?" Grandpa had expressed an interest in his friend, Monica, a collectibles appraiser, months ago. "Why aren't you on a date this evening?"

He gave an overdramatic gasp. "What do you mean? I thought I was having a date with my two best gals!"

I laughed. "Well, that's true. But I'm talking about Monica. I thought you liked her."

"I do like her," he said. "But since she leased a space in Shops on Main, it's a little touchy. If we go out and decide we don't like each other, I still run the risk of seeing her every time I come to visit you."

"Her shop is upstairs, and I'm on the lower level," I said. "That excuse doesn't hold a lot of water."

"Ford is upstairs, and I see him all the time. Jason is upstairs."

That was true. Jason's photography studio was in the same building as Designs on You.

"Exactly," I said. "If I'm not afraid to put myself out there with a guy I'll have to work in the same building with if things fall through, then you have no excuse."

He shrugged. "I'll think about it."

"Should we talk about the elephant in the room?" I asked.

"You mean the two elephants who are coming up here from Florida in the next day or two?"

"Yeah." I rubbed the bridge of my nose. "It'll be weird having them back in the house. I mean, I didn't take over their bedroom or anything, but I'm used to having my privacy now."

"You've become pretty set in your ways, have you?" he asked.

"I just—" I trailed off, not knowing how to finish the sentence.

"I know, Pup. I know." He stood. "What do you say we go inside and get that pizza started?"

"Sounds good to me."

The three of us went inside, and Grandpa gave Jazzy a can of her favorite cat food while I tied an apron on over my clothes.

Before we could get started cooking, though, Max sent us a video chat request. I put my phone on a stand so she could see us—and vice versa—while we worked.

"Hi, Max," I said.

"Hello, beautiful," Grandpa said.

"Hello, darlings. Get a load of this." Max raised her hands up to the sides of her head. "'Double, double toil and trouble! Fire burn and cauldron bubble!'" She laughed and lowered her arms. "Is that spooky, or what?"

"That's pretty spooky," Grandpa said.

"I see you've been reading Macbeth." I washed my hands at the kitchen sink before chopping peppers to go on our pizza.

"I have. I think I'm going to try that bit out on Zoe the next time I see her. What do you think?"

"That might not be the best idea," I said. "She seemed to get a little freaked out at Cross's Antiques today."

While Grandpa browned ground beef in the skillet, I told him and Max about our visit to the shop.

"Wait," Max said. "An antique shop gave her the heebie-jeebies even though she knows *me*? That doesn't make sense."

"She was not only convinced the place was haunted, but she didn't like the needlepoint portrait I bought at all."

"Let's see it," Grandpa said.

"I left it in the car. I'm going to take it into the shop on Monday and clean it up a bit. No offense to Ms. Cross, but that shop is pretty dusty."

"Cross's Antiques..." Grandpa's voice was so low it was hard to hear him over the sizzle of the beef. "That's the place to the right of Cassie's shop, isn't it?"

"Yes."

"If I'm not mistaken, my granddad used to tell us a ghost story about that place when we were little." As if realizing what he'd said, he whipped his head around to look at the phone.

"Don't worry, silver fox. I'm not offended." Max winked.

"I never heard any stories about you," he said quickly.

"Rats. That is insulting." She made a pouty face. "Spread some tales around about me, won't you?"

He chuckled and turned back to the skillet.

I finished chopping the peppers and got to work on the onions. "Go on, tell us what you heard about Violet Cross's shop."

"All right. There was a cabinet maker who worked in the shop—he and his family lived above it. This was back in—oh, I reckon it was the late 1800s. Anyway, his oldest son didn't want to follow in the father's footsteps, and he went to work on the railroad."

"Ooh, did he go west, young man?" Max punctuated her question with a raised fist.

"Actually, no," Grandpa said. "He went to work on the railroad right here in Abingdon. Unfortunately, he died in an accident while they were clearing the rail beds, and it's said that Thomas Wortley haunts the building to this day." With a sigh, he removed the pan from the stove and turned off the eye. "I'm sorry, Max. It was thoughtless of me to tell that story."

"It was my fault," I said. "I'm the one who told you Zoe thought the place was haunted."

"Don't apologize to me." Max scoffed. "I'm not that thin-skinned. In fact, I enjoy hearing ghost stories." Once again, she raised her arms. "'By the pricking of my thumbs, something wicked this way comes.'" She laughed. "Huh? Doesn't that give you the willies?"

I laughed, but for some reason, it did give me the willies.

Chapter Three

Grandpa called me early Sunday morning. "Hi, Pup. You awake yet?"

"Um..." I stifled a yawn. "Sure."

"Sorry. I didn't mean to wake you, but I didn't want you to be blindsided if you turn on the news—Violet Cross was found dead in her shop last night."

"What happened?" I sat up, now fully alert.

"She was murdered. Her son went to check on her when he was unable to reach her by phone yesterday evening. The shop was in disarray, but authorities haven't determined what, if anything, was taken."

"Grandpa, let me call Zoe and tell her before she sees it on the news. I'll call you right back."

"No need. I'll see you when you get here."

Jazzy and I almost always had Sunday lunch with Grandpa. After ending our call, I phoned Zoe.

"Hey." Zoe's answer was clearer and more responsive than I was expecting it to be this early on a Sunday morning.

"Hi, there. Have you seen the news?" I asked.

"No way. I avoid that garbage at all costs. Why? What's going on?"

"Violet Cross was found dead in her shop last night."

"The nice old lady we met yesterday?" Zoe changed her tone. "She told you to get off her lawn? That's weird, *Stacy*."

Ah.

Zoe didn't want her mother, Maggie, to know she and I were talking. Maggie was okay with Zoe working at my shop now, but she didn't want us being too close. She felt I was a bad influence on her daughter because I'd managed to get myself involved in a couple of murder investigations. And she didn't even know about Max. Zoe said her mother would have a conniption and forbid her working at the shop if she ever found out there was a ghost living there.

"I'll talk with you later," I said.

"Yep. Later."

Jazzy and I got to Grandpa's house at around one o'clock. I'd watched the news coverage of Violet Cross's murder online. It was appalling. I hadn't known Ms. Cross terribly well, but she was a sweet person. She'd have given anything in her store to someone she thought needed it. And I felt sure she'd have handed over the money in the register without the robber needing to be violent. Her murder simply made no sense.

Grandpa and I had decided on today's menu before I'd left last night. I supposed that was kind of gluttonous of us to plan lunch while we were still full from supper, but we tried to live by the motto of: Fail to plan or plan to fail.

Walking into the house, I could smell Grandma Jodie's meatloaf in the oven. Although she'd been gone for five years, Grandpa still followed her recipe to the letter. It made us both feel closer to her when we enjoyed that meatloaf.

After letting Jazzy out of her carrier, kissing Grandpa on the cheek, and washing up, I asked, "What do you need me to do?"

As if it had been scripted, there came a knock at the door.

"I need you to answer the door, Pup." He was standing at the sink washing a bowlful of potatoes.

I chuckled. "Be right back. Wait. Mom and Dad didn't say anything about arriving early, did they?"

"Not to me. Your guess is as good as mine as to when they'll show up."

Trying to peep through the front glass, I was surprised to see a flash of blue—as in, Zoe's shade of blue hair. I opened the door to Zoe and her papaw, Dwight. "This is a surprise."

"Ain't it a hoot?" Dwight gave me a hug when he came through the door. "Zoe put this here application on my phone, and it lets me ask somebody to come pick me up and drive me somewhere. Since I haven't had a driver's license in eight years, I thought we'd give it a go. We tested it for the first time and came here. It worked!"

"That's terrific," I said.

Zoe shrugged, but she looked rather pleased with herself. She had her papaw wrapped around her little finger, so I imagined she realized that this opened up new avenues for her as well as for him.

"What smells so good?" Dwight asked.

Grandpa came out of the kitchen drying his hands on a tea towel. "It's lunch. Y'all are just in time. Or you will be when it's ready."

"What needs to be done?" Dwight was walking toward the kitchen.

"Come chat with me while I peel these potatoes," Grandpa said.

"Chat, my eye. I'm a whiz at peeling potatoes." Dwight spotted Jazzy. "Little Jasmine! How nice to see you!"

The cat came and rubbed against his leg.

"Zoe, would you like to learn to make biscuits?" I asked.

"I guess."

We joined the men in the kitchen, and I got out the flour, baking powder, sugar, salt, butter, and milk. I spread a sheet of wax paper on the counter and got out the biscuit cutter.

"This looks hard," Zoe said.

"I know, but it's not." I smiled, as I set the oven to preheat and took the cookie sheet out of the drawer beneath the oven.

Grinning as he peeled a large potato, Dwight said, "I can't tell you how glad I am to see you all. I enjoy video chatting, but it's not like seeing people in person."

"No, it's not." I felt a twinge of guilt over not going to visit Dwight more often. "I've been meaning to stay sometimes when I drop Zoe off, but—"

"Oh, now, I understand," Dwight said. "The house has been in an uproar through all these renovations. Things are finally getting manageable again."

"Plus, Mom is a tyrant who doesn't want us to have any friends," Zoe said.

"We're together now—that's what matters," Grandpa said.

Handing Zoe a measuring cup and a mixing bowl, I instructed her to put two cups of flour into the bowl.

"Poor Ms. Cross," she murmured, making me doubly glad for the wax paper as she poured flour all over the countertop. "Who'd want to rob her place? Everything in there looked like junk to me."

"I think antique shops are like treasure hunts," I said. "You have to be willing to sift through the dirt and rocks to get to the gold."

"Amanda's right," Grandpa said. "Ms. Cross's murderer was likely looking for something specific."

"That, or somebody had a grudge against her." Dwight put the peeled potato into the bowl and got out another.

"Maybe it was the ghost," Zoe said. "Not all ghosts are awesome like Aunt Max."

Grandpa and I shared a look. I gave a slight shake of my head to dissuade him from mentioning the ghost reputed to haunt Cross's Antiques.

"You're going on the assumption there is a ghost there," I said. "From what I saw of the news reports, officers at the scene are certain their suspect is human."

Zoe rolled her eyes.

"Max can't touch anything, remember," Grandpa said. "She can only use the tablet because it's electronic."

I brightened, delighted that Grandpa Dave had come to my rescue. Why had I ever doubted him? "That's right! Only yesterday she told us she wished she could hug us."

"Yeah, but can't ghosts have unique abilities?" Zoe asked. "We living people can't do all of the same things. Why should it be different for them?"

None of us had a satisfactory answer for that.

At home later, I was curled up on the sofa looking through a book on old Hollywood style when my phone rang. Seeing Jason's name pop up on the screen, I decided to adopt a sultry voice, a la Lauren Bacall.

"Hello," I said.

"Oh, sorry," he said. "Did I wake you up?"

"No. I was being funny."

Too late, he forced a laugh. "Have you had a nice day?"

Sobering, I said, "Well..." I went on to tell him about Violet Cross being found dead at her shop hours after Zoe and I had visited.

"I heard about that on the news this morning," he said. "That's terrible."

"It is." I realized I hadn't spoken with him yester-day. "My mom and dad are coming for a visit later this week."

"Nothing like giving you plenty of notice, huh?"

I chuckled. "Maybe they were afraid if they gave me more notice, I'd schedule a trip out of town."

He joined in my laughter, this time confident I was joking. I wasn't entirely certain I was kidding.

"I hope I get a chance to meet them," Jason said. "I mean, if you want me to."

"Of course, I do." I'd met his parents, and I certainly hadn't made a stellar first impression, but I was sure my parents would be delighted with him. Still, it was going to be tough enough to be judged on my shop without adding my love life to the mix. "I know how terribly busy you are right now, though. If you're unable to get together with them during this visit, they'll have something to look forward to the next time they come to Abingdon."

"You know I'll make every effort to get together with them."

"I know." I smiled. "What are you working on this evening?"

"A set of proofs from a wedding I did last week." He sighed. "I've fallen behind a little, but I'll get there."

"I have no doubt you will."

After speaking with Jason, I put the book away and retrieved my laptop and my sketchbook. He'd reminded me I had my own work to do—namely, the sketches for the Macbeth costumes.

Logging into my favorite search engine to look for other costume renderings, I saw another article about Violet Cross's death in headlines the search engine thought would be of interest to me. I forced myself not to click on the link. But even as I scrolled through images of Macbeth, my mind wandered back to the robbery and what Grandpa Dave had said about the killer searching for something specific. What on earth could it possibly have been?

Chapter Four

As I walked from the parking lot to the building on Monday morning, I had Jazzy's carrier in one hand and the needlepoint portrait in the other. Luckily, Connie arrived immediately after I did and was able to unlock and open the door for me.

Connie owns Delightful Home, the boutique across the hall from Designs on You.

"Thank you," I said.

"My pleasure. What have you got there?"

"It's a needlepoint portrait I bought on Saturday at...at Cross's Antiques."

She gasped. "Oh, my goodness! You must've been one of the last people to see poor Violet alive."

Putting Jazzy's carrier onto the floor, I unlocked the door to Designs on You. "Did you know her well?"

"Not really." Connie pushed a strand of her honey-blonde hair behind her ear before picking up Jazzy's carrier and following me inside the shop. "I guess it's more accurate to say I was acquainted with her. She sometimes came here to buy essential oils and organic tea blends, and I loved visiting her shop."

"Me too." After closing the door and letting Jazzy out of her carrier, I walked through to the workroom where Jazzy's divided dish awaited. "I can't imagine such a horrible thing happening to Ms. Cross. She was so tiny and frail—she must've been terrified."

"I'm sure." Connie followed me into the atelier and ran her hand lightly over a bolt of blue silk. "Nobody would refer to me as tiny or frail, but I would've been scared to death."

There was a woodpecker-fast rap on the door leading from my shop to the kitchen. Before I could open it, Ella and Frank joined us.

"We heard your voices," Ella said. "Do you know about what happened to Violet Cross?"

"We do," Connie said. "We were just talking about it. Did you know Violet?"

"No, we never met her," Frank said.

Frank and Ella owned Everything Paper, the other shop on the lower level of Shops on Main. They were an older couple, and I'd have thought they were acquainted with Ms. Cross too. Maybe they didn't like antiques and/or Ms. Cross didn't care for stationery supplies.

"That's beside the point." Ella wrung her hands as she paced. "If it happened to her, what's to keep it from happening to us?"

Jazzy meowed up at me impatiently.

"Excuse me a moment please." Leaving Connie, Ella, Frank, and Jazzy in my workroom, I picked up Jazzy's dish and slipped across the hall to the kitchen.

"What's going on?" Max demanded from her perch atop the refrigerator. "Who's Violet Cross?"

"I'll explain as soon as everybody goes about their business," I whispered, filling one side of Jazzy's dish with water.

"What are you whispering about?" Ford asked, walking into the kitchen with his coffee mug. He glanced around the room. "Better yet, who are you talking to?"

"Sorry, Ford. I'm already frazzled this morning."

"Is it because of Violet Cross?" He began making a pot of coffee.

Nodding, I put some kibble into the other half of Jazzy's dish. "Feel free to join us for the worry-fest."

"All right." Ford finished preparing the coffee-maker before going across the hall and opening the door for us both.

Max floated down from the fridge and into the room ahead of the proprietor of Antiquated Editions and me.

"Ford, what do you think?" Frank asked. "Ella seems to believe we're all going to be set upon by thieves and murderers, but I feel that what happened to Violet Cross was an isolated incident. Let's hear your opinion."

Ford stroked his beard. "While I'm inclined to agree that the robbery and murder of Ms. Cross is an anomaly, we must be vigilant. If any of us sees any-one behaving suspiciously, we should let the others know immediately."

"That's a good idea," Connie said. "We should set up a text group so we can quickly communicate with everyone in the building at once."

I placed Jazzy's dish by her bed, and she happily ignored all the drama in the room. I half wished I could do the same.

"That's easy for you to say, Ford," Ella said, craning her neck looking up at the burly bookseller. "You're upstairs. Whether we text you or not, you'll be fine. You'll hear the gunshots and hide or something."

"Violet wasn't shot," Connie said. "Or, if she was, the news report I heard didn't mention it. That report stated she'd suffered a blow to the head."

That's what I'd read as well, but I couldn't get a word in edgewise to agree with Connie.

"Just because Violet Cross was bashed on the noggin doesn't mean one of us won't get shot," Ella said. "They robbed and killed her, and they got away with it. The thieves are going to think all mom-and-pop operations are vulnerable now."

"We are," Ford said. "And don't say I'm not every bit at risk as everyone else here simply because my shop is upstairs. How would I escape a killer, Ella? Jump out the window?"

Trish Oakes, Shops on Main's manager, opened the door. "What is all the commotion about? I could hear you the instant I walked in. Is this the welcome with which we aspire to greet our customers?"

"You know it's not," Frank said. "We're all on edge about what happened at Cross's Antiques over the weekend, and we're wondering what security measures we can take."

"Oh." Ms. Oakes relaxed her expression slightly. "That was indeed horrendous, and I understand your anxiety. However, we have an excellent alarm system, and nothing gets past our security cameras."

"I do," Max said. She was sitting on the file cabinet swinging her legs. "At least, I think I do. Is there any way we can check and see?"

Ignoring Max's question, I said, "The alarm system and security cameras are great when we aren't here, but I believe we'd all prefer to feel safer while we're in the building."

"Right," Ella said. "Thank you, Amanda." She looked at Ms. Oakes. "Is there any chance of our getting a security guard? Maybe he or she could set up a post in the middle of the hall."

"I'm afraid we don't have the budget for that," Ms. Oakes said.

"I can do it." Frank looked at his wife. "You shouldn't have any trouble managing the store on your own—at least, until Violet Cross's killer is caught."

"I'll be happy to help when traffic is slow in my shop." Ford clapped Frank on the shoulder.

"And I'll give Amanda the scoop if I see any suspicious palookas hanging around," Max said.

"Thanks," I said.

"Yes," Connie said. "We appreciate you, Frank—and you too, Ford—for helping us feel more at ease."

"It's settled then. Good." Ms. Oakes nodded. "Everyone be vigilant, and I trust this storm will blow over quickly." She opened the door and left.

Ella poked her tongue out at Ms. Oakes' retreating back.

Max laughed. "Go, Ella!"

Frank put his arm around Ella. "You know I'll do whatever it takes to protect you."

Connie and I shared a smile. Who knew Frank could be such an old Prince Charming?

"I smell fresh coffee," Ford said. "Anybody else here need some caffeine?"

"I do," Frank said.

"Me too." Ella followed the men out of the room.

Connie shook her head. "Where were we before the call to arms?"

I chuckled. "You were getting ready to look at the needlepoint portrait I left in the reception area."

"Oh, yeah," Max said. "Zoe says it's icky, but I want to judge for myself."

I retrieved the portrait and placed it onto the worktable. "It's awfully dusty."

"Isn't it gorgeous though?" Connie leaned closer. "Look at the thousands of tiny stitches."

"Why, that's not icky!"

"It's not icky at all," I said. Darn it, Max.

"Of course, it isn't." Connie frowned at me in confusion.

"I'm sorry, Connie. Zoe was with me when I bought the portrait on Saturday, and she tried to talk me out of getting it. She said it was icky and that it was probably haunted or something."

Laughing, Connie said, "Kids and their wild imaginations!"

"Right? She even thought the antique store was haunted. I mean, just because we—" I stopped abruptly, and Max grinned and clapped her hands. "—we're always hearing that every old building in Abingdon has at least one ghost doesn't make it true."

"To give credit where credit is due, the ghost of Thomas Wortley does supposedly roam about the antique shop, that is, if you go in for ghost stories," Connie said.

"Please don't tell Zoe that," I said. "I'll never hear the end of it."

"Understood." Connie looked back at the portrait. "I'd take this to the dry cleaner if I were you. I wouldn't try to clean it myself. It's too delicate."

"You're right. That would be the safer option."

"Well, I'd better get across the hall and open the shop." Connie affected Ms. Oakes' tone. "Being absent is not the welcome with which we aspire to greet our customers."

"Who is Thomas Wortley?" Max asked as soon as Connie left. "Is he on the computer?"

"I doubt it, but we'll see if he is." I opened my laptop and did a search for Thomas Wortley + 1890. Going on what Grandpa Dave said about Thomas Wortley working for the railroad, that seemed like a good year to start.

To my surprise, there was a write-up in a local archived newspaper about Thomas Wortley's death in 1897. A photo accompanied the article.

"Oh, my goodness."

Looking over my shoulder, Max said, "And how! He's almost as handsome as Hugh Allan."

"That's not what I meant. This same photograph was framed and displayed behind the counter at Cross's Antiques."

Chapter Five

I took the needlepoint portrait to the dry cleaner at around eleven a.m. that morning, since I wanted to be back during many people's normal lunch hour of noon until one p.m. Since the weather was warmer, a lot of folks enjoyed walking downtown on their lunch break and browsing the shops.

On the way back, I went by Abingdon Gifting Co. to talk with Cassie. Lucky enough to find a parking spot on the street near her shop, I parked and went inside.

Cassie was standing at the counter in the back of the store working on a gift basket. From the yellow bunny and baby items, I guessed it was for an expectant mom.

"How sweet!" I walked closer to get a better look at the basket's contents.

"Thanks." Cassie smiled, but she seemed subdued.

"I'm so sorry about Ms. Cross," I said.

She closed her eyes for a moment and then blinked back tears. "I still can't believe it. Violet was such a character. Who could do—?" She shook her head.

"Obviously, I didn't know her like you did, but she did seem to be a character. When Zoe and I went to the shop on Saturday, Ms. Cross had a framed photo of Thomas Wortley on a shelf behind the counter. Was she related to the Wortley family?"

"No." Cassie smiled slightly. "As weird as this sounds, I think Violet had a crush on Thomas Wortley. I'd visit her shop sometimes after closing up here, and she'd be talking with someone even though there was no one else in the shop. I'd ask her who she was talking to, and she'd say, 'Thomas.' Then she'd laugh, but I got the impression she wasn't always joking."

"She was probably having a little fun with you. And judging by her photo, Thomas was a pretty nice-looking guy."

"Yeah, well, I'd have thought she was being funny if it had only happened once. The second or third time, I began to worry that maybe Violet was getting dementia or having an adverse reaction to some new medication or something. I even spoke with her son, Jack, about it."

"Do you think the rumors about Thomas Wortley haunting the antique shop could be true? Or that maybe Ms. Cross thought they were?"

Squinting at me over top of the basket she was still stuffing, Cassie asked, "Are *you* having an adverse reaction to some new medicine?"

I laughed. "I don't believe so."

"Something weird did happen one night when Scott and I were here setting everything up for the Bubble Bar," she said, speaking of her husband. "It was after midnight, and we heard this clacking noise. I asked him, 'What's that?' He said it sounded like somebody hitting the keys on a manual typewriter."

"What did you do?"

"We went home. The next day we both felt foolish over it; but at midnight, it was scary."

"I imagine so," I said. "But didn't Ms. Cross live above her shop? Maybe she had insomnia and was catching up on her correspondence that night."

"Maybe." She got some cellophane to wrap the basket.

"Did you ever ask her about it?"

"No." She spread the cellophane onto the counter. "I didn't want her to think I was a nosy neighbor."

"You must think I'm horrible then." It didn't matter to me if Cassie thought I was too inquisitive or not—I wanted some answers. "What about Jack? Did he say he'd make sure Ms. Cross's medicines weren't causing any side effects?"

"Yeah, but..." She waffled her hand back and forth. "He didn't seem to care much one way or the other. Hopefully, he was having an off day or something, and I read him wrong; but he acted like checking on his mother was a burden."

"That's sad." I began wandering around the shop. "I need to find something for Frank Peterman. He's playing security guard until Ms. Cross's killer is caught. This whole thing really has everybody at Shops on Main edgy. I can only guess how nervous you must be."

Clack, clack, clack, clack, clack, clack, clack. Ding!

Slowly turning toward Cassie, I asked, "Did you hear that?"

"I thought I was imagining it."

"If so, we're having some sort of shared hallucination."

Clutching the scissors she'd used to cut the cellophane, she asked, "Do you think it's the killer?"

I thought it was more likely the ghost, but I didn't dare say so. "Why would the killer be typing?"

"I don't know. Maybe he's writing out his confession. Should we call the police?"

"Let me go out front first and peep through the window to see if there's anyone in there," I said. "If I see any sort of movement, we'll call the police."

"All right, but—good grief, girl—be careful. I've done lost one friend this week."

"I will." I didn't expect to see anything—why would Ms. Cross's killer be so brazen as to return to the scene of the crime in the middle of a workday?

Walking outside and taking the few required steps to Cross's Antiques, I cupped my hands to the glass and peered inside. I didn't see any movement inside the shop, but I nearly jumped out of my skin when an elderly woman yelled at me.

"Rubbernecker! You ought to be ashamed!"

"But I—"

"You disgust me!" she interrupted me before ambling on down the street.

"I thought someone was inside!" I called to the woman. When she didn't respond, I returned to Cassie's shop. "I didn't see anything, but now somebody thinks I'm a horrible person—maybe more than one somebody, given all the cars stopped for the traffic light."

"Don't worry about it," Cassie said. "I heard the woman yelling at you and saw that it was Mrs. Willoughby. She thinks everybody is horrible."

"Well, whatever we heard probably wasn't coming from Cross's Antiques," I said. "Our imaginations were probably playing tricks on us."

I didn't really think so, and judging by Cassie's half-hearted "maybe," neither did she. Still, she retrieved some ribbon for her basket, and I went back to looking for a treat for Frank.

Clack, clack, clack, clack, clack, clack, clack. Ding!

This time, I got goosebumps.

"Maybe it's Ms. Cross' son?" I shrugged. "Could the noise be coming from upstairs?"

Cassie opened her register and took out a key.

"What're you doing?" I asked.

"Violet and I have keys to each other's back doors just in case something might happen and one of us would need to get into the other's shop. Let's go see if Jack is in there. If so, I can give him this key and get mine back."

"All right." I didn't know if we were feeling emboldened because there were two of us or if it was because I hadn't seen anything going on inside the shop and we were eager to prove to ourselves there was nothing going on. Either way, Cassie and I hurried next door to have a quick look around.

Cassie unlocked the back door to Cross's Antiques and slowly pushed it open. She stood back as if she expected someone—Ms. Cross's killer, most likely—to come barreling out.

"Want me to go in first?" I asked.

"That's up to you." She made no effort to move.

Had I not been acquainted with Max, I'd have been hesitant to go inside as well; but I honestly thought—hoped—that if it was the ghost, he was merely trying to tell us something.

I stepped over the threshold and immediately felt a blast of cold air. Had Cassie not been with me, I'd have spoken to Thomas Wortley. Since she was, I asked, "Anyone here?"

"Jack!" Cassie called. "Is that you, Jack?"

Glancing around the shop, I spotted the typewriter. I didn't want to venture into the area where Violet Cross might've been murdered.

"There's no one here," Cassie said. "Let's go back."

"All right."

Clack, clack, clack, clack, clack.

I shuddered, and Cassie gripped my arm.

"We have to get out of here," she whispered.

"Not until we take a look at that typewriter."

Eyes widening, Cassie asked, "Are you insane?"

"No. It's going to keep happening until we check it out," I said, my breath coming in shallow pants.

"What if the killer is using that typewriter to lure you farther into the shop?"

"Then he's invisible, and we don't have a chance against him anyway." I looked around. "Do you *see* anyone?"

"No." She bit her lip. "Maybe you were right the first time. Maybe the sound is coming from upstairs." She raised her eyes to the ceiling. "Jack! Are you up there, Jack!"

Since there was no response from upstairs, I moved closer to the typewriter. "Stay there. I'll be fine."

"I'll come with you." She took the scissors from her pocket. "At least, I'm somewhat armed."

When we approached the typewriter, I saw a sheet of paper in it. Had that been there on Saturday? I couldn't recall.

Again, I felt cold, and I shivered. Not only because of the possible presence of the ghost, but because of what was written on the paper.

Find out who killed Violet.

The phrase had been written over and over.

Cassie crept closer. "What does it say?"

As we watched, more words were typed onto the page:

I won't rest until I know... and neither will you.

With a scream, Cassie fled the shop.

"Thomas, is that you?" I asked softly.

Yes.

"I'm sorry I can't see or hear you, but I'll do my best to find out who murdered Violet. Did you see anything that day that might help me? Anything I can tell the police?"

No. I failed her.

"You didn't," I said. "I'm going to take this paper. Is that all right?"

Put in new paper. Behind the counter.

"Um...I don't want to walk where—"

You won't. My poor Violet died at the foot of the stairs leading up to her apartment.

"I'm sorry," I whispered. "I'm so sorry."

I went to the counter and, with trembling hands, got a fresh sheet of paper. After removing the one Thomas had nearly filled, I inserted the paper into the typewriter.

Not knowing what else to say, I left to go do the hard part: convince Cassie to help me.

Chapter Six

After calling Grandpa Dave and asking him to meet me at the shop, I stopped and got sandwiches for the two of us. He was waiting for me in the parking lot when I arrived.

Striding toward my car, he asked, "Is everything all right, Pup?"

I got out of the car, and Grandpa put his hands on my shoulders and carefully examined my face.

"I'm fine. I've had quite a morning, though." I opened the hatch of my car and got out Frank's basket."

"Is that for me?"

"Not this time." I went around and got the sandwiches from the passenger side of the car.

"Thank goodness," he said. "I was afraid I'd either forgotten some occasion or was about to be bribed."

"Bribed?" I grinned.

"Hey, with your parents coming in, it was a reasonable assumption."

"True," I said. "But it would look really bad if you and I suddenly remembered that vacation we'd planned. Right?" I laughed. "Just kidding. I'm honestly looking forward to their visit...sorta...but their timing couldn't possibly be worse."

"What aren't you telling me?"

"I'll explain everything once we're inside alone. This basket is getting heavy."

We walked into the building where Frank, sitting at a card table in the hallway, never glanced up from his word-search puzzle book. I felt safer already. Nothing was going to get past our gatekeeper.

"Hi, Frank," I said.

He started. "Oh, hello, Amanda...Dave. I heard your vehicles pull in." He raised a hand that still held his mechanical pencil. "I didn't want to disturb you though. I think my being as unobtrusive as possible is the key to making everyone feel that they can go about their business as usual."

"Well, this is for you." I handed him the basket. "It's a token of appreciation for your willingness to protect us all."

"Now, that wasn't necessary." He hurriedly removed the bow from the basket. "I do appreciate it, though, and I'll leave it on this table in case Ford comes down and takes a turn at guard duty." He snagged two packets of cookies from the basket. "Thank you."

"You're welcome," I said. "We'd better go eat our lunch."

"Good seeing you, Dave," Frank said. "Stop back by for a chat before you leave if you have time."

"Will do," Grandpa said.

I swung by the kitchen to get a couple of soft drinks. When I got to the workroom, Max was filling Grandpa in on why Frank was pulling guard duty.

"Gracious," he said. "I had no idea everyone here was so concerned about their safety. Is that why you called me, Pup?"

"Not exactly." I spread some paper towels over a section of the table. "And I don't believe all the vendors are worried. Monica and Jason weren't at our impromptu vendors' meeting this morning, and both Frank and Ford said they believed Violet Cross's death was an anomaly. Still, better safe than sorry, I imagine."

"But Ford also said you're all vulnerable," Max pointed out.

"That's true, but it's not why I need to talk with you." I pulled a chair over to the table and took a seat. "I met Thomas Wortley a little while ago."

"What?" Grandpa pulled a chair over beside mine. "You mean, an ancestor?"

I shook my head.

Rubbing his chin, he said, "I was afraid that seeing Max might make you more sensitive to the paranormal."

"Was Thomas a doll like in the photo?" Max asked.

"I didn't see him. It's more accurate to say I communicated with him." I took a deep breath and told Grandpa and Max everything that had happened after I'd walked into Abingdon Gifting Co. Afterward, I took the folded paper from my pocket and handed it to Grandpa.

Max read it over his shoulder. "Aw...he loved that woman."

"Did you show this to Cassie?" Grandpa asked.

"I did. She said no way will she ever go back into that shop again, but she'll keep the key handy so I can communicate with Thomas. Or she will unless Violet Cross's son asks Cassie to return the key."

"Isn't that the bees knees?" Max raised her clasped hands to her throat and twirled. "He wants justice for the woman he loves."

"Maybe so," I said, "but I feel it's unfair of him to threaten to haunt Cassie and me if Ms. Cross's killer isn't found."

Max stopped twirling. "If he's tethered to that building like I am to this one, then he could really only haunt Cassie."

"Max has a point." Grandpa unwrapped his sandwich. "Although that's not good either."

"And, if you think about it," Max continued, "you're already being haunted for all intents and purposes—by me. You don't seem to mind that."

"But you're my friend," I said.

"Well, let that dreamboat sail right on over here," Max said with a grin, "and I'll be his friend too."

There was a knock on the atelier door before Monica Miller poked her head inside. "Hi. May I join you?"

"Of course," I said.

Max scoffed. "Her—he can haunt. The rest of us will be a happy little bunch of bananas."

I wasn't sure whether Max genuinely disliked Monica or was simply piqued by what Monica represented to her—a living person with an interest in Grandpa who might somehow take Max's place in our lives. I'd told her repeatedly that would never happen—that she was irreplaceable—and I'd pointed out that Zoe had grown our family rather than hampered it. But she had correctly pointed out that Zoe and Dwight were her biological family and could see and interact with her. Most other people could not.

Monica sat at the end of the table and spread a paper towel out before opening her container of salad. "Thank you for allowing me to join you. I hate eating alone."

"Anytime." I smiled. "Did Ford fill you in on why Frank is posted in the hallway?"

"No, but Trish Oakes did. She thinks everyone is blowing an isolated incident out of proportion." She shrugged. "I say, if it makes some people feel safer, what harm can it do?"

"Did you know Violet?" Grandpa asked.

"I'd been in her shop a time or two, but I wouldn't say I knew her." Monica drizzled a packet of raspberry vinaigrette dressing over her salad. "I found her shop to be extremely disorganized."

Max floated behind Monica's head and mocked her. "Blah, blah, blah extremely disorganized blah, blah. My shop is perfect, as is my little salad."

I looked at Grandpa, who was trying to hide a grin.

"As a collectibles appraiser, what do you think the killer might've been looking for in Violet's shop?" he asked.

"Absolutely nothing!" Max said, still pretending to be Monica. "If they want anything of value, they need to rob me!"

Monica shrugged. "Could've been anything."

Max was being difficult to ignore, but I managed to do it. "My friend owns a shop in the same building as Cross's Antiques. I was there today, and we heard a manual typewriter. We went over there to check it out, but there was no one there." I didn't dare tell Monica what Cassie and I had discovered. Keeping my tone light, I asked, "Have you ever come across any haunted objects while doing your appraisals?"

She laughed. "Hardly. I've encountered people who imagine they have haunted or enchanted objects, but we all know that's a load of nonsense, don't we?"

"Oh, really?" Max put her hands on her hips and glared at Monica. "I wish I could dump that salad over your head—you'd see what a load of nonsense it is."

"You think it's possible?" I asked. Okay, so ignoring Max wasn't easy at all. I quickly turned my head to Grandpa to pretend I'd been talking to him.

"I believe there are a lot of things in this world that can't be explained," he said. "Whether or not that includes a possessed typewriter is beyond my powers of speculation."

"I'm guessing you heard something else and attributed it to a typewriter," Monica said. "It could have been something as simple as a woodpecker or someone hammering. I'm sure the tragedy happening next door to her has your friend on edge—and you too, for that matter."

Max mimed picking up the salad, dumping the bowl onto Monica's head, and rubbing it into her hair like an orange on a juicer.

"Not to change the subject," I said, "but I bought a needlepoint portrait at Cross's Antiques on Saturday. It's at the cleaners now, but I'd love to get you to appraise it. Not because I want to sell it or anything, I'm simply curious."

"I'd be happy to appraise the piece for you. Bring it up when you get it back."

"Thank you."

"It's a gorgeous day out," Grandpa said, apparently hoping to wade into safer waters than talk of ghosts and haunted typewriters.

As he and Monica discussed the weather, my mind wandered back to the possibility of Thomas Wortley haunting the object rather than the shop. After all, I couldn't see or hear him. If his spirit were inside the typewriter, I could offer to buy it and bring it here. Then we could communicate more frequently, and he could tell me everything he knew about Violet Cross's murder. Or he could become increasingly frustrated with my efforts and more easily haunt me, since he'd be in my shop.

Chapter Seven

Not long after lunch, Selma and Stuart Greenfield came to look at the costumes I'd sketched for them. For Lady Macbeth, I'd designed an emerald boatneck gown with gold and burgundy tippets on the trumpet sleeves. The Macbeth tartan provided trim at the collar and waist, and I'd further embellished the neckline with jeweled medallions. Even though Max wasn't in the shop at present, she'd already expressed her delight with the gown. I only hoped Selma Greenfield would be as excited as my ghostly fashionista friend.

"Oh, this is beautiful," Mrs. Greenfield said, "but could you do the gown in blue rather than green? Everything else can stay the same."

"Of course. Would you want a light blue, indigo, navy...?"

"Indigo, I think. Stu?"

"Yes, yes. That would be wonderful, dear," he said.

I noted on my sketch to make the gown indigo, rather than emerald.

Mr. Greenfield's costume was an undertunic in burgundy with a sleeveless, floor-length overtunic in the same shade as Mrs. Greenfield's gown. The overtunic was trimmed with gold brocade, and there was a sash of Macbeth tartan to be worn over his left shoulder and secured with a thistle brooch.

"I'm guessing you'll want to change Mr. Greenfield's overtunic to the same blue as your gown," I said.

"Definitely." Mrs. Greenfield smiled at me and then at her husband. "You'll look so handsome!"

"And you, my queen, will be breathtaking." He raised her hand to his lips.

I wondered if Max would find the man's actions noble or nauseating. I thought it was a little over the top, but to each his own.

"If you're ready to move forward with the costumes, I'll need to get your measurements," I said.

"Absolutely." Mrs. Greenfield stood. "Lead the way."

While I was logging Mrs. Greenfield's measurements, Zoe and Dwight arrived. I stepped out from behind the Oriental privacy screen that served as my fitting area to tell them I'd be with them soon.

"No problem," Zoe said. "We'll keep Mr. Greenfield company."

That girl was an absolute treasure.

"That was your assistant?" Mrs. Greenfield asked.

"Yes—Zoe."

"I thought I recognized her voice. I really wish we could convince her to be a fairy princess for the Faire."

I chuckled as I measured the span of Mrs. Greenfield's shoulders. "Zoe isn't quite the princess type. She might show up as some sort of fairy warrior, though."

"That would work. I'll talk with her about it while you're measuring Stu."

When I finished up with Mrs. Greenfield, I took her husband back to the fitting area.

"Zoe is an enterprising young woman," he told me, as we stepped behind the screen. "She was asking me what sort of hats sell well at RenFaires. Is she an aspiring milliner?"

"She is. Over the Christmas break from school, she made dozens of cloches which I allowed her to sell here in the shop. They were quite popular."

He smiled. "Already an entrepreneur at her age. I like that. I myself started young. I had a lawn mowing business."

"That's hot, tiresome work," I said.

"It is. But I appreciated every dime I got from it— and in those days, I didn't get much more than a dime." He laughed.

I heard someone come into the shop, but knowing Zoe was there, I didn't go out. Instead, I pulled the measuring tape around Mr. Greenfield's chest.

"Who are you? I thought this was my daughter's shop."

Hearing that loud, sharp voice, I told Mr. Greenfield, "Please excuse me for just one second. I'll be right back."

I stepped out from behind the screen to find my mother standing in the reception area with her hands on her hips. Dad was happily introducing himself to Mrs. Greenfield, Dwight, and Zoe.

"Hi." I gave Mom a quick hug. "Hey, Dad!"

"Hello, Princess!"

"I'll be with you in just a minute." I hurried back to finish Mr. Greenfield's measurements.

"Well!" My mother was obviously ticked. "We shouldn't have even bothered to come. She doesn't care if we're here or not."

"Of course, she does," Dad said. "But she has a business to run. We can't expect her to drop everything on a whim."

"On a whim?" She huffed. "She knew we were coming in."

"We didn't give her a specific time."

I was mortified that my parents were arguing on the other side of the screen where I was trying to concentrate on taking accurate measurements. Aware that Mr. Greenfield couldn't help but hear them as well, I tried to ease the tension.

"Have you and Mrs. Greenfield done the Renaissance festivals for a long time?" I asked.

"Um...y-yes, yes, for quite a few years," he said. "You know, I'd be happy to return at a more convenient time."

"There's no time like the present." I forced some brightness into my voice. "I'm eager to get these measurements done so I can start on your costumes. I'm really excited about them."

"So am I. You did a marvelous job on the designs."

"I refuse to be treated like this," Mom said loudly. "I'll be in the car when you're ready to leave."

Although I wished the floor would open up and swallow me, I smiled at Mr. Greenfield and asked him to hold the tape measure at his waist while I stretched the other end to his ankle.

When I finished the measurements, and Mr. Greenfield and I returned to the sitting area, I didn't see Mom. She must've made good on her threat to wait in the car.

Dad was talking up a storm with Mrs. Greenfield, Dwight, and Zoe.

He gave me a warm hug when I walked over to him. "I'm so proud of you! These designs are fantastic!"

"Thank you." I could feel myself blushing at his praise.

"We're delighted with Amanda's designs and cannot wait to see the finished results," Mrs. Greenfield said. "Right, Stu?"

"You bet!" He looked at his watch. "My lady, hadn't we better be going?"

"Why?" She frowned, but then her expression cleared. "Oh, right. Amanda, dear, we'll look forward to your call about the first fitting."

"I'll get to making these costumes right away."

As soon as Mr. and Mrs. Greenfield left, I dropped the smile and turned to Dad. "Did Mom really go pout in the car?"

"Probably." He shrugged.

Strolling in from the atelier, Max looked at Dad, smiled, and said, "Hiya, handsome. Is that broad of yours jingle-brained or what?"

Dad laughed. "Did Amanda make your costume too? It's great."

My eyes widened as I looked at Zoe. Like Dwight, she was too busy watching Max and my dad to notice me.

"No, darling." Max spread her arms and looked down at her mauve dress. "These are the duds I was wearing when I fell down those steps out in the hallway."

I squeezed my forehead with both hands and knew I'd need some aspirin before the day was out.

"Dad, this is Maxine Englebright. I call her Max."

"And Papaw and I call her Aunt Max," Zoe said.

"Pleased to meet you, Max. Call me David." He stretched out his arm to shake Max's hand.

"We can't touch Max," I said. "She a ghost."

He grinned. "Sure, she is. How did you plan this when we didn't tell you exactly when we were coming?"

"I'm around here pretty much all the time," Max said.

"I wanted you to meet Max, Dad—just not like this," I said.

"Sorry, darling," Max told me. "I was going to wait and let you formally introduce us. But then your mother threw her tantrum, and I hoped I could help lighten the mood."

By this point, I was thinking maybe something stronger than aspirin would be necessary. Especially when Dwight decided to pitch in his two cents.

"We all think the world of your daughter," he said. "It was she who brought us together with my deceased Aunt Max—my mother's sister."

"Is your mother still living?" Dad asked.

"Oh, no. She's been gone for twenty years or more," Dwight said.

Dad looked around the room. "And is she around here somewhere too?"

"No. Just Aunt Max."

"But she's the elephant's eyebrows," Zoe said, "and we love her to pieces."

"As far as we know, we—Dwight, Zoe, Grandpa Dave and I...and now you—are the only people who can see and hear Max," I said.

"Uh-huh." He was nodding, but he still wasn't buying it.

"You left out Jasmine," Max said. "She can see me. Oh, and those awful little weasels Joey Conrad brings in here can see me too."

Jazzy got out of her bed at the sound of her name, came to sit on the floor near Max, and pawed the air.

"Watch," Max said.

As she floated around the room, Jazzy followed her before dropping to the floor and rolling onto her back.

"How are you doing that?" Dad asked me.

"I'm not. Really. Ask Grandpa."

Mom barged back into the shop. "David, are you coming or not?"

"Hi, Mom," I said.

She glared at me. "Oh, you're going to acknowledge my presence now?"

"I'd like you to meet Dwight and Zoe," I said. "Zoe assists me in the shop, and Dwight is her grandfather."

Barely sparing them a glance, she said, "Nice to meet you. I'd like to go to the house and get settled in now."

"Aren't you going to introduce Max?" Dad asked.

"Is that its name?" Mom looked down at Jazzy, who'd stood now and was walking toward her.

"No, that's Jasmine—Jazzy, for short." I tried to catch Dad's eye to give him a silent warning, but he wouldn't look at me.

Max went over to Mom. "What's your problem, Toots? Is your corset too tight? You need to loosen up!"

Dad laughed. "Yeah, Toots. Lighten up!"

Mom glared at him. "Excuse me?"

"I was just agreeing with the ghost," he said.

"The ghost." She rolled her eyes. "Already you two are sharing inside jokes."

"Oh, I'm no joke," Max said. Turning to us, she added, "I'll pop back in when she leaves."

And then Max was gone.

Dad's jaw dropped. "Wh-what? Wait, how'd you do that, Amanda?"

"Do what?" Mom heaved a sigh. "I want to go to the house, and I want to go now."

After fishing in his pocket and producing the car keys, he tossed them to her. "Go ahead. I'll wait and come home with Amanda."

"Fine." Once again, Mom stormed out of the shop.

"Did she even look the place over?" I asked.

Zoe shook her head. "I owe you an apology."

I remembered her saying no way was my mother worse than hers. She'd apparently now reconsidered. I wasn't keeping score, though; I was wondering how I was going to explain the unexplainable to Dad.

Chapter Eight

After Mom left, I sent a video chat request to Grandpa Dave.

"Hey, Pup," he said brightly when he'd accepted my request. "Miss me already?"

"Of course, but...I'm here with Dad." I moved the phone around to show him Dad, who was sitting on one of the navy wingback chairs clutching a bottle of water.

"Oh, hey, son! When did you get in?" Grandpa asked.

"A few minutes ago," Dad said.

"Where's Terri?"

"She left."

Grandpa's eyes sought mine.

"I've already made her angry," I said.

"That woman's behavior was inexcusable," Max said.

I could see from our tiny image in the corner of the screen that Max's head appeared to be on my right shoulder.

"What—?"

"That doesn't matter at the moment," I interrupted Grandpa. "Right now, Dad is freaking out over the angel on my shoulder."

He laughed. "Are you sure about that designation?"

Max wagged her finger. "Be nice, silver fox."

"I've tried to explain that you and I can see and communicate with Max because your maternal grandfather was the love of her life and that Dwight and Zoe can interact with her because they're her blood relations," I said. "But I believe he's still convinced her being here is some sort of an elaborate prank I've concocted."

"My mom could probably see Max too," Zoe said, "since she's Papaw's daughter, but we won't let that happen."

"No." Dwight shook his head. "Maggie isn't terribly open-minded about some things, and she'd freak out at the thought of Zoe working in a haunted building—even if the one doing the haunting is a beloved relative."

"How can I help you make sense of all this, son?" Grandpa asked.

"I'm not sure you can. I'm stunned that all of you take Max's presence in stride."

"I have to admit I was afraid I'd gone off the deep end when I first realized not everyone can see Max," I said. "She told me she was a ghost, but I had to go get Grandpa so he could confirm that he saw her too. It was only when Grandpa could see and communicate with Max too that I was convinced she wasn't a figment of my imagination."

"Really?" Max placed a hand on her chest. "Do you honestly think you could have dreamt up an imaginary friend this fabulous?"

Dad pinched the bridge of his nose. "Let me make sure I'm understanding this correctly. You—all of you—communicate with a ghost on a daily basis, and you're okay with that?"

"Sure, we are." I shrugged. "We love Max."

"Aw, right back at you!" She looked at Dad. "These ducks brought joy back into my existence, David. They even made it possible for me to read and to enjoy shows. And even though I can't leave this building, I can go places with the help of this tablet.

It allowed me to see Zoe's school's production of *Beauty and the Beast* a few months ago. Let me tell you, it was spectacular."

Dad studied her for a moment. "You seem nice...intelligent...normal..."

"I'll take nice and intelligent," Max said, "but never call me normal."

I laughed and then motioned for Zoe to follow me into the atelier.

"I feel like Grandpa is the one who can really help Dad accept Max," I said.

She nodded. "Your grandpa is super cool."

"So's yours. Mr. Greenfield said you'd asked him about hats sold at the Renaissance Faire. He was impressed with your drive and entrepreneurial spirit."

Smiling and looking down to hide her pinkening cheeks, she said, "Mr. Greenfield is kinda cheesy, but he seems nice. He told me the most popular hats and headpieces sold at the festivals are daisy crowns, circlets, pirate hats, musketeer hats, muffin hats, and Tudor French hoods."

"All right. Now let's narrow that list down to things it will be easy for you to make and sell," I said.

"I had time to look up circlets, and they look easy," she said. "I could probably make those with the jewelry wire you get in craft stores."

"Let's see if you can—I've never made a circlet before." Since Dad, Dwight, Max, and Grandpa Dave were making use of the tablet, I used my phone to search the internet for instructions on making circlets using jewelry wire. "Wow, look at this." I turned the phone around to show Zoe all the instructional videos I'd found.

"Those are beautiful," she said. "Given the instructions, I can make those."

We likewise found tutorials for making daisy crowns, felt pirate's hats, and muffin hats. There were a couple of instructional blogs for making Tudor French hoods and musketeer hats, but we both felt they might prove to be too difficult and not as profitable to sell as the others.

While it was still only the two of us, I decided to tell Zoe about my earlier experience with the ghost of Thomas Wortley. After I'd finished the story, I said, "I thought you should know."

"That's so cool! Can we go back and talk with him?"

"Maybe," I said. "Like my Dad with Max, I believe my encounter with Thomas Wortley is something I'll have to sit with for a little while before I can get up the nerve to approach him again. I mean, Max is different—we know her."

"But it's like Aunt Max said—the guy loved Ms. Cross, and he wants to avenge her death."

"Yeah." I smiled and changed the subject. "Let's make a list of everything you'll need to start on your hats, and I'll take you to the craft store tomorrow after work. I can't do it today because I should probably get home."

"Don't worry about it." Zoe flicked her wrist. "After we get the list made, I'll get Papaw to take me to the craft store. He's totally loving what he calls the taxi app."

I laughed. "Yeah, well, it's getting too late to go today anyway, so Dad and I will drive you home. You and Dwight can save the taxi app for tomorrow."

"You're planning on hiding from your mom for as long as you can, aren't you?"

Nodding, I said, "You'd better believe it."

When Zoe and I returned to the reception area, I asked Dad if he'd like to meet the other vendors.

"Are they all living?" he asked, with a wink at Max. He'd come a long way over the past half hour, although I wasn't a hundred percent convinced he didn't still believe Max to be some sort of elaborate hoax.

"You wouldn't know it to look at some of them," she said.

"Zoe, if you'll hold down the fort, then Dad and I will drive you and your papaw home when we get back."

"Consider it held," she said. "I'll even straighten up the atelier."

"Thank you." I looked at Dad. "She's an incredible help around here. I dread when school starts back at the end of August."

First, I took Dad to meet Connie.

"Connie, I'd like you to meet my dad, David," I said. "Dad, this is Connie."

"What a pleasure to meet you." He shook her hand, making the thin bangles on her wrist jangle. "I've heard wonderful things about you and Delightful Home."

"And I've heard magnificent things about you from both your daughter and your father." Connie smiled. "They're both highly thought of here at Shops on Main." She went to her tea blends and got a tin of kava. "For you. Hopefully, it will help soothe your nerves after traveling all day."

"We've actually been travelling for two days," he said. "Thank you."

She stopped him before he could pull out his wallet. "The tea is a gift to welcome you."

"That's awfully kind," Dad said. "I look forward to trying this."

"It's delicious," I said. "And it really is relaxing."

Next, we went down the hall where Frank was still sitting guard.

"Hi, Frank," I said. "I'd like you to meet my dad."

Frank stood and shook Dad's hand. "Frank Peterman. Nice to meet you."

"David Tucker, likewise."

Squinting, Frank said, "I can see it. You favor your dad."

"I'll take that as a compliment."

Frank took a couple of steps toward Everything Paper. "Ella! Come out here and meet Amanda's daddy!"

"I'm not in Kalamazoo, dear," Ella said, as she strode out of the shop. "I'm Ella Peterman." She shook Dad's hand. "We're all ever so proud of Frank for vowing to protect us from any hooligans who might come around. Amanda here even brought him a gift basket from her friend Cassie's shop. Wasn't that nice?"

"It was." Dad looked at me. "Where's my gift basket?"

"Welp, Ella, you've done gone and got the young 'un in trouble," Frank said.

"He'll get a gift basket when he volunteers for guard duty," I said, with a grin. "We're going up to meet Ford before he leaves."

Dad reiterated to Frank and Ella that it was nice to meet them both before going up the stairs to Antiquated Editions. As a lover of books, Dad was more interested in Ford's shop than in anyone else's in the building—with the possible exception of mine.

I heard Trish Oakes leave as Dad was browsing Antiquated Editions and talking books with Ford. Oh, well, he could meet Ms. Oakes tomorrow. Jason hadn't been in today; and since I hadn't told Dad much about Monica Miller, I didn't care if he waited until tomorrow to meet her too. I wondered if Mom would even come tomorrow and look around the shop or if she'd continue to pout. I could never be sure with her.

We'd left Ford's door open, and Monica came over before we left.

"I'm heading out and wanted to say good evening." Her green eyes regarded Dad with open curiosity.

"Monica, this is my dad," I said.

"Dave's son." She smiled broadly. "It's a pleasure to meet you. Dave and I have known each other for quite some time, and in fact, it was he who helped me find this charming building."

"I'm sure I'll be back tomorrow," Dad said. "I'll enjoy looking over your shop then."

"Thank you. I'll be happy to show it to you," she said. "I'm quite proud of it."

"As well you should be," Ford said.

Hearing Monica's footsteps fading on the stairs, Ford nodded toward Jason's studio. "Have you met the boyfriend yet?"

"No." Dad folded his arms across his chest and arched a brow. "Give me the dirt on him."

I supposed I'd better grin and bear it while the two of them teased me about Jason.

"He's a good-looking fella, if you go in for that tall, dark, athletic type." Ford spread his hands. "And he seems to be nice enough—respectful, hard worker. I keep an eye on him."

"Good to know," Dad said.

We heard footsteps on the stairs.

"If I'm not mistaken, here comes our hero now." Raising his voice, Ford said, "'And we loved with a love that was more than love...'"

"I and my *Amandabel* Lee," Jason said.

Laughing, I stepped out of Ford's shop.

"I figured it was you he was talking to." Jason placed his equipment on the floor and held out his arms.

I ran to him and let him lift me up into his arms. He twirled me around before kissing me.

Dad cleared his throat.

"Go away, Ford," Jason muttered playfully.

"I'm not Ford. I'm David Tucker."

Jason's eyes widened. "Really?"

I nodded. "Go away, David Tucker."

"She's kidding," Jason said quickly, letting me go and hurrying to introduce himself to Dad.

"I'm not so sure she *is*," Dad said. "She's always been incorrigible, and it appears you're encouraging her." He nodded toward the equipment. "I understand you've been shooting a lot of weddings."

"Yes, sir. And engagement photos."

"You do excellent work. I saw the photo of Amanda that hangs over her mantel."

"Sometimes a photographer is only as good as his subject," Jason said, looking down at me.

"It's a pleasure to meet you," Dad said. "We need to get home and see if her mother got us unpacked and settled in, but I'd love to take you to dinner one evening while we're here so we can get to know each other better."

"I'd enjoy that too."

As I followed Dad down the stairs, I was delighted that he got to meet Jason; but I couldn't help but imagine how ticked Mom was going to be that Dad was the life of the Shops on Main party while she was at home pouting. The fact that it was her own choice was beside the point. She had a habit of overlooking anything that didn't suit her.

Chapter Nine

As we drove toward home after dropping Dwight and Zoe off at their house, Dad said, "I like Jason. Your grandpa had already given me his seal of approval, of course, but he's not usually as critical as I am."

Even though I was happy that Dad had liked my boyfriend, I knew I was pressed for time. We'd be home in fifteen minutes, and who knew when I'd get him alone again?

"Dad, something happened earlier today." Then, as quickly as I could, I filled him in on Violet Cross's death and my communicating with the ghost of Thomas Wortley through an antique typewriter.

"If I hadn't already met one of your spooky pals, I wouldn't believe you." He leaned his head back and closed his eyes. "Are there any other ghosts in your life I need to know about?"

"Not that I know of. The only reason I'm telling you about Thomas Wortley is because he asked me to help discover who killed Ms. Cross." I braked at a STOP sign and put on my left turn signal.

Opening his eyes, Dad said, "Don't go home yet. We'll pick up dinner first."

"Thanks." I knew he was buying us more time to talk. "Even if Thomas Wortley hadn't threatened to haunt Cassie and me—which I hope was an empty threat—I still feel compelled to a least keep tabs on the investigation into Ms. Cross's death. Who else could or would communicate with the guy?"

"I'm dreaming, right?" Dad asked. "I'm going to wake up in a few minutes and find I've been asleep in front of the television, and that's why I've been dreaming about flapper ghosts and unsolved murders and..." He trailed off.

"I know it's a lot." I expelled a long breath. "Believe me. I know. This morning with the typewriter? That shook me to my core."

Gayle Leeson

Taking my hand, Dad said, "I'm sorry. After the whole Max thing, I thought you'd become accustomed to supernatural experiences."

"I'm used to Max now—for the most part. But I wasn't expecting to communicate with anyone else's ghost today. Or ever."

"Neither was I."

"I know it's crazy, but you'll get more comfortable being around Max. It's completely strange at first; but if you accept the fact that she's only a person who...well, who happens to be dead, you'll see that she's sweet. And loads of fun."

"Why does she haunt the building?" he asked.

"She died there, but she doesn't know why she's still there. She isn't always. It takes a lot of energy for her to be present with us." I shrugged. "Her existence at Shops on Main is an enigma, even to her. One thing's for certain though. We can't tell Mom about Max."

"Absolutely not. She'd have us both committed."

"I'm not going to talk with her about Violet Cross's murder either, if I can help it," I said. "I can't guarantee she won't hear some of the other vendors discussing it. As you could likely tell from Frank's being posted in the hallway, several of them are pretty concerned about it."

{ 98 }

"You don't honestly think there's a thieving killer out there targeting small businesses, do you?"

"No. I believe Violet Cross's murder was personal. It didn't even appear that anything was taken from her shop."

"I wouldn't worry about it then. The police will get to the bottom of it."

Keeping my eyes on the road, I asked, "What are you thinking for dinner?"

"You aren't seriously considering looking into this woman's personal life yourself, are you?" he asked.

"What did I say to give you that idea?"

He frowned. "It's not what you said. It's how you didn't say what you said...or didn't say."

"That doesn't make any sense."

"It makes perfect sense, and you know it," he said.

It actually did. He was telling me that what I didn't say spoke volumes. We had a knack for reading each other.

"I'll do the bare minimum to keep my promise to Thomas Wortley, okay?"

"Why?" He raised his hands. "Why can't you simply stay away from Cross's Antiques and let the detectives—the real ones—do their jobs? Eventually, they'll catch her killer, and Thomas What's-his-name can rest in peace."

"And if that doesn't happen?" I asked.

It was his turn to avoid giving a response. "Chicken would be good, don't you think? Maybe we can get Dad to join us."

"That'd be great. Give him a call," I said. "But before you do, will you promise to help me with Mom?"

"You know I'll do the best I can."

I smiled. "That's all I ask."

Grandpa arrived at my house—still technically Mom and Dad's house—just as we did. I figured he'd designed it that way. If not, he was the luckiest man on the planet. Not that Mom would've been unfriendly to him, but I was guessing he didn't want to deal with her alone knowing she was already in a foul mood.

I got out of the car and retrieved Jazzy in her carrier from the back seat. Dad carried the bag with the bucket of chicken, tubs of macaroni and cheese and mashed potatoes, and the box of rolls.

Grandpa gave my shoulder a reassuring squeeze as we stepped onto the porch.

Dad walked into the house first. "Terri, we're home, and we've brought dinner."

"I'd have been happy to cook had I known what to prepare." She shot me an accusatory glance. "Not that there's much here to make."

I let Jazzy out of her carrier. "I don't do a lot of cooking when I'm going to be eating alone. When I plan a meal, I buy what I need on the day I'm making a particular dish. I don't waste food that way."

"And when we eat together, we usually cook at my house." Grandpa kissed Mom's cheek. "How are you, Terri?"

"Fine, I suppose. How are you?"

"Finer than frog's hair." He winked at me. "That chicken sure does smell good."

"Doesn't it though? I'll feed Jazzy and then wash my hands and set the table."

"I'll set the table," Mom said.

As I fed Jazzy, I wondered how long Mom and Dad planned on staying. Probably not long, since Dad would have to go back to work. That thought—and the relief it brought—pricked at my soul. I'd love to have Dad here all the time, but Mom and I were like oil and water. Around her, I always felt I never could do anything right.

When I joined everyone else at the dinner table, Dad and Grandpa Dave were talking about the vendors at Shops on Main.

"I've come to know and like them all," Grandpa said. "I knew you and Ford would hit it off."

"He has some incredible books, including some signed first editions. I plan to go back tomorrow."

"Are you sure those signed first editions aren't fake?" Mom asked. "There are some awfully shady people in this world."

"Of course, I'm sure. He has the certificates of authenticity and their provenance or chain of ownership." Dad poured us each a glass of sweet tea. "I'm not sure I can afford any of them, but I want to look at them again."

"Here I wanted you to be proud of my shop, and you've fallen in love with Ford's," I teased.

"Your shop is incredible," Dad said. "That's a mighty nice shelf you've got in your workroom." He grinned at Grandpa. "Looks like something built by a master carpenter."

"Thank you, son. Your endorsement check is in the mail."

"He's actually got a lot of business from that shelf," I said. "You know, Connie from Delightful Home?"

Dad nodded. "The bohemian, earth mother type who gave me the tea."

"Right." I took a biscuit from the box. "She had Grandpa replace the cabinets in her kitchen after seeing the shelf he made me."

"So, did you meet everyone in the place today?" Mom asked Dad.

"Everybody except the building manager," he said, spooning macaroni onto his plate.

"You can meet her tomorrow." I took the macaroni Dad passed to me.

"She's a little prickly," Grandpa said, "but she's not bad."

"You'd have gotten a kick out of Ford when he heard Jason coming up the stairs," Dad told Grandpa.

"Jason? Mandy's boyfriend?" Mom put down her fork and leveled her gaze at Dad.

"Yeah." He either didn't foresee or chose to ignore the brewing storm. "Ford started quoting from *Annabel Lee*—"

"Jason is used to Ford spouting love poetry to us, by the way, which is why he took it in stride," I said.

"That was apparent," Dad said. "He came back with the quote I and my *Amandabel* Lee. It was pretty clever, although I wasn't about to tell him that."

"I thought you told us he wasn't going to be in the building very much this week, Mandy."

"He isn't," I said. "He only came in today to pick up a lens he needed for a shoot he's working on tonight. He comes and goes. I never know when he's going to be in the building right now because he's doing all these weddings and engagement shoots."

"Well, I do hope David and I will get to have a proper introduction to him while we're here," Mom said. "Over dinner or coffee, at the very least."

"We'll try, Mom. But as I said, this is Jason's busiest time of the year."

"Mmm, this chicken is juicy," Grandpa said. "Thank you for inviting me. Tell me all about your drive up from Florida."

I hid a smile. My hero. Max would be so proud of the silver fox for helping me dodge Mom's slings and arrows.

Chapter Ten

I got up early on Tuesday morning, and Jazzy and I left the house before Mom and Dad woke up. The building was eerily quiet when we went into Shops on Main, and since it was barely daylight, I locked the door behind me. The clicking of my heels on the hardwood floor echoed as I walked into my shop.

"I hope this place isn't haunted!" I called, as I unlocked the door going into the atelier.

I was surprised when Max didn't respond. Of course, she wasn't present all the time. But I'd wanted to talk with her this morning before everyone else arrived.

After letting Jazzy out of her carrier, I went into the kitchen to prepare her breakfast and to put on a pot of coffee. Opening the refrigerator for a bottle of water, I gasped when I saw Max scrunched up with the top shelf seemingly intersecting her sternum.

"What? You weren't expecting to find a juicy tomato in the fridge?" She laughed. "I thought I'd make like your mother and give you the cold shoulder."

"Ha-ha." I took a bottle of water from shelf in the door and shut the refrigerator before carrying Jazzy's breakfast and my water into the atelier.

Max got there before I did and was sitting on the floor with Jazzy. "I'm sorry. I didn't mean to be insensitive—I only wanted to make you laugh. Your being here this early seemed like a bad omen."

"Not really. I simply have no idea what the day will bring, and I wanted to ensure you and I got some time to talk."

"Aw, that's swell. Thanks."

"Last night wasn't the best, but it wasn't a total disaster." I told Max about dinner and how Grandpa Dave had helped keep the conversation light. "Naturally, Mom was ticked because Dad got to meet everyone, including Jason, and she didn't."

"That's her sack of potatoes—let her carry them. She's the one who got vexed and behaved like a bratty child."

"True. But I'll have to take her around the building today and listen as she gushes to strangers about how proud she is of me after she wouldn't even take an interest in my shop yesterday."

"You don't believe she'll be too embarrassed to pull some phonus balonus like that?" Max asked.

"Never. She'll strut around like the queen of the manner." I opened my water bottle and took a long drink. "After Grandpa left last night, I apologized to Mom and told her—"

"*You* apologized? For what? Darling, she owed you the apology. She was rude to you in front of your clients."

"I know, but Mom never apologizes. I knew I'd have to make the first move if I wanted their visit home to be a pleasant one."

Max moved from the floor to the worktable, and Jazzy went to eat her breakfast.

"Let's go into the reception area," I said.

I went through, unlocked the reception door, sat on one of the two navy wingback chairs in front of the window, and slipped off my shoes.

Tucking my feet under me and resting my head against the back of the chair, I said, "I told Dad about Thomas Wortley."

Lowering her form onto the chair beside mine, she shook her head. "Why? Hadn't the man had enough of a shock already?"

I shrugged. "I guess I was thinking in for a penny, in for a pound. Plus, I'll need his help keeping Mom in the dark."

"I wouldn't imagine that to be a problem. She struck me as the type of person who believes what she wants to believe, and everyone else is wrong."

"That's accurate." I chuckled. "But I want to avoid as much grief from her as possible."

My cell phone rang.

"So much for avoiding grief," Max murmured.

I fished my phone out of my deep skirt pocket and looked at the screen. "It's Cassie." I answered the call. "Hey, there, are you okay?"

"No. That infernal typewriter is driving me up the wall. He was typing when I left yesterday; and as soon as I got here this morning, he started up again," she said. "Please do something. Please."

"I'm sure if you went over there and just talked to him—"

"Do I look like the Long Island medium to you?" she asked.

"Okay, okay. Stay calm. I'll be right there."

"Go," Max said, as I ended the call. "I'll keep Jazzy company."

I used Cassie's key to gain access to Cross's Antiques. Walking through the back storeroom, I could hear the typewriter keys.

Clack, clack, clack, clack, clack, clack, clack. Ding!

"Calm down, Thomas. I'm coming."

I made my way to the typewriter to see what he'd written.

Jack, Jack, Jack, Jack, Jack...

Those four letters nearly filled the page.

"What about Jack?" I asked.

He has been in here a lot.

"So? This was his mother's store. Why wouldn't he be in here? He needs to sort out her things, decide—"

I was interrupted by Thomas's typing.

He keeps looking for something and muttering to himself.

"What's he saying?"

I don't know. I was a railroad worker, not a linguist.

"Great. Another sassy ghost." I sighed. "Jack is speaking a foreign language?"

He might be. Why do you trouble me with so many questions when you should be speaking with him?

"I'll talk with Jack. In the meantime, please stop driving Cassie insane with all your typing."

Lucky you—able to talk. I need clean paper.

"A little kindness wouldn't hurt. I'm sure your mother taught you good manners."

Please. Happy now?

"Yes. I'll talk with you as soon as I know something."

Thank you.

I took Cassie her key back. "I asked him to stop making you crazy and said I'll talk with him again as soon as I know something."

"How can you be so calm about communicating with a ghost?" she asked.

Shrugging, I said, "Maybe I think this is all a dream?"

"A nightmare is more like it, and I'm right there with you. What did he want anyway?"

"He said Jack has been over there a lot and that he's searching for something. Thomas doesn't know what he's looking for. Has Jack mentioned anything to you?"

"I've been so busy I haven't spoken with Jack since Sunday after I heard about Violet," she said. "I need to call him."

"Why don't we go and see him today after work? I'll stop on the way and buy a pie or a casserole or something."

"What are you planning to do?" She paced the floor in front of the counter. "You aren't going to tell him about the possessed typewriter, are you?"

"Of course not. We're expressing our sympathy for the loss of his mother—that's all." I placed a hand on her shoulder. "Hopefully, this will all be over soon."

"If taking Jack Cross a pie makes that happen, I'll get him one in every flavor."

I returned to Shops on Main with a box of glazed doughnuts. Taking the treat into the kitchen to leave for everyone, I saw Ford getting himself some coffee.

"Well, aren't you a ray of sunshine?" he asked. "Just in time for me to enjoy a doughnut with my coffee. Your parents are here, by the way."

"What?" I looked out the window. "I didn't see their car in the lot."

"They must've parked out front then. Your dad is upstairs with me, and—" He looked around. "I'm not sure where your mom is."

"She's snooping around the shop," Max said.

"Super," I said.

Ford chuckled at my exasperation. "Aw, it's all right, kid. I'll tell your dad there are doughnuts down here."

"Thanks, Ford." I went into the atelier, but Mom was in the reception area occupying the wingback chair I'd been sitting in before I was summoned to ghost duty. "Good morning, Mom."

"Hello. Where've you been? Do you always leave your shop unlocked?"

"Normally, I lock my shop, but I only stepped out for a moment. I brought doughnuts for everyone. They're in the kitchen."

"I thought you liked these people." She scoffed. "You bring them the unhealthiest breakfast on the planet?"

"Yeah, well..."

"Ooooh!" Max stormed across both rooms to stand in front of Mom. "I'll have you know I'd love to have one of those delicious-looking treats! And Ford was happier than a cat with two tongues with his!"

*A cat with two tongues...*that was new. I slowly joined Mom in the reception area. "Ford told me dad is upstairs in his shop."

"Yes, and if you're wondering where your *boyfriend* is, check this out." She turned her phone's screen around to me.

"What's that?" I asked.

"It's a video." She turned it back toward herself and hit play. "I was doing a little checking up on your Jason Logan on social media, and I found this." She held the phone out to me.

I took it reluctantly. With Max peering over my shoulder, I watched as some pretty bridesmaid flirted with Jason and then wrote her phone number on his hand.

"Oh, I know what that was," Max said. "I bet I know what that was. I know *exactly* what that was!"

"Well, *what?*" I was addressing Max. Mom didn't know that, of course, but the question still worked.

"*What?*" Mom demanded. "Some beautiful girl is giving your boyfriend her phone number, that's what. And by the look on his face, he's planning on calling her. This *is* your boyfriend, isn't it?"

"Well, yeah, he's going to call her...b-because...she...is a *client*!" Max nodded triumphantly, obviously delighted she'd been able to come up with a fairly reasonable alternative to a flirtatious couple making a date.

"She could be interested in his work, Mom," I said.

She snorted. "I imagine he's interested in *her* work, too."

"Now you hold on!" Max shouted. "You don't know what's going on in that movie! None of us do!"

"It's okay," I told Max...and Mom. "I trust Jason."

"Fine. I just hope you're not getting played for a fool," Mom said.

Dad walked into the shop munching on a dough-nut and carrying a cup of coffee. "Hey, Princess! Thanks for the doughnuts. How thoughtful." He came over and kissed my temple. Sensing the tension in the room, he asked, "What? Did I miss some-thing?"

"Not a thing, Dad." I smiled. "So how rich are you getting ready to make Ford?"

Chapter Eleven

Thankfully, the shop was busy, despite it being a Tuesday morning. Our busiest days were typically Fridays and Saturdays and sometimes Mondays—especially when children were out of school on break. And while I always welcomed browsers, new clients, and favorite patrons, I was especially grateful for their presence while my parents were here. I wanted Mom and Dad to see that my shop was successful.

Dad had gone upstairs to Antiquated Editions after finishing his doughnut and washing his hands. He now returned with an autographed first edition of *The Greatest Success in the World* by Og Mandino.

Holding it up proudly, he said, "Check it out! Well, from a distance. Neither of you can touch it."

I laughed. "Oh, please let me touch it."

He clutched the plastic-wrapped book to his chest. "Never."

"Haven't you read that book already?" Mom asked.

"This book isn't for reading, Terri. It's for having. It's a collectible." He looked at me. "Ford has a copy of Hemingway's *For Whom the Bell Tolls* that I have my eye on, but I'm not sure I should get it."

"If you don't, you're going to regret it," I said.

"Pursue your dreams, darling," Max had suddenly appeared at his side.

"Whoa," he said. "I didn't know you were there."

"I wasn't until now," she said.

"You didn't know who was there?" Mom asked.

His eyes widened.

"Jazzy," I answered for him. "She always stays in here, Dad. That's why it's important to keep the doors closed all the time."

"Good thinking, sweet child-o-mine."

I laughed and looked at Max. "I'll have to play you that song later." Yikes. It's harder than I thought to be with one person who can see Max and one who can't.

"You haven't introduced me to the other vendors yet," Mom said.

"Hopefully, we can do that after lunch," I said.

"Where are we going for lunch?" she asked. "What do you usually do?"

"I usually bring something from home or grab a granola bar and eat it at my desk." I watched as she rolled her eyes. "But we can do whatever you'd like. You haven't been home for a while."

"Let me know what you two decide," Dad said. "I'm going to go back and look at that Hemingway a little more."

He took his Mandino with him. He must've been serious about that no-touching policy.

"I'll give lunch some thought." Mom stood and stretched. "In the meantime, I'll go visit the shops and introduce myself."

"Mom, if you'll let me order the Macbeth tartan and thistle brooch for my clients' costumes—"

Sighing, she said, "Do whatever you need to do. I'll wait. Some more." She dropped back onto the chair.

There was a brief knock at the door before a cheerful woman with deep dimples breezed into the shop.

"Good morning!" Her eyes danced as she took us all in.

I liked her immediately. "Welcome to Designs on You. I'm Amanda. How may I help you today?"

"My friend Selma Greenfield said I simply must come to see you if I wanted a costume for the Renaissance Festival." She held out a hand. "I'm Imelda. Imelda Stanbury but please call me Imelda."

"It's a pleasure to meet you, Imelda," I said.

"Am I interrupting?" she asked. "I'm more than willing to wait my turn."

"Of course, you aren't interrupting. This is—"

Before I could get the words out, Mom got up and flounced out of the reception area, leaving the door standing open behind her.

"This is a perfect time," I finished.

Max stuck her tongue out at Mom's retreating back. "I'll follow to see what she's up to."

Hurrying over to shut the door, I certainly didn't want to let on to Imelda that the diva who'd just left was my mother. I pushed the chair Mom had been sitting on over to the desk. "What sort of costume are you looking for?"

Imelda sat on the chair and raised her hands to her cheeks. "I want to be a wise woman." She giggled. "I know it sounds silly, but it's what I want."

"It doesn't sound silly to me at all." I got out my sketchbook and colored pencils. "I believe we can make you a lovely wise woman costume. Do you have something in mind?"

"I was thinking one of those red corset dresses." She held her hands slightly out from her sides. "Think you can get all this laced up?"

"I'm sure I can," I said, with a chuckle. "What about something like this?" I sketched out a cream chemise with trumpet sleeves and a corseted overdress in red. "And since you're a wise woman, what if we make you a hooded cloak?"

"That would be marvelous! I'll look like a cross between Little Red Riding Hood and her granny!" She laughed.

"You'll be beautiful." I added the cloak and a small basket with a handle. "Of course, I can't make the basket, but—"

"I'll find one." She grinned. "Measure me up."

"You're pleased with the costume the way I've drawn it here?" I asked.

"Absolutely."

I ushered Imelda behind the privacy screen and took her measurements. "You're in luck. I was getting ready to order the supplies I need for the Greenfields' costume, and I can go ahead and order yours too. I'd be happy to see what sort of baskets I can find if you'd like."

"I'd love for you to," Imelda said. "I'm entrusting this entire costume to your expertise."

After I'd measured her, she browsed the ready-to-wear pieces for a few moments and then left with a broad smile and a wave goodbye.

I sat at the desk, opened my laptop, and after adding the items for Imelda's costume to the cart where I already had the Greenfields' accessories, I placed my order.

Dad returned through the atelier door and scooped up Jazzy. He wandered through to the reception area and over to the desk. He nodded at the sketchbook. "That's neat. Is someone having a costume party?"

"Renaissance Festival," I said. "I'm doing Lord and Lady Macbeth too."

Connie gave a tap on the door before she came into the reception area. "Hi!" She encompassed both Dad and me in her smile. "I met Terri. She's very nice."

"I sense a *but* coming," I said.

"Well..." She grimaced. "She was wondering why Frank was sitting in the hall, so I explained that some of the vendors have been on edge since the death of a shop owner at the other end of town. I'm sorry. I thought she was aware of Violet's death."

"Don't think another thing about it," I said. "In fact, I should've told her."

"I'm still sorry to have been the bean-spiller."

"Thanks again for that kava tea," Dad said. "I really enjoyed it, and I slept like a baby last night."

"You're welcome," Connie said. "I'm going to go through Amanda's atelier and into the kitchen for some coffee. Having the kids home for the summer is wonderful, but we have a tendency to stay up too late at night because they don't have to get up early the next morning."

"That makes it awfully hard on Mom," Dad said.

"It does...but, you know, I wouldn't miss out on this time with them for anything."

"I understand completely. You'll even feel that way when they're grown." He looked at me. "Maybe even more so."

As Connie left, Max popped in near the desk. "Aw, how sweet! You know, David, had you and Connie been Amanda's parents, she'd have been this plucky, free-spirited gal who'd have designed gowns with ostrich plumes."

Dad laughed. "For one thing, Connie is too young to be Amanda's mom, and two, I'm glad she has Terri as a mom because I think Amanda is perfect the way she is."

"Thank you," I said. "But now I feel compelled to create a gown embellished with ostrich feathers."

"Do it, darling," Max said. "It'll be marvelous."

I looked up dresses with ostrich feathers and turned the laptop around to share the results with Max and Dad. Dad was showing us how some of the women in the gowns might walk—complete with his arms folded into wings—while Max and I laughed until we were in tears.

"Goodness," Mom said, barging through the door. "I could hear you two all the way out in the hall."

"Close the door, dear," Dad said.

She pushed the door closed and asked, "Amanda, why didn't you tell me about the murder of the woman at the antique shop?"

"I didn't want to worry you. Besides, it's my feeling that Violet Cross's death was an isolated incident."

"That's not what Ella Peterman thinks." Before Mom could elaborate, two middle-aged women came in to browse my ready-to-wear line. Mom looked pointedly at her watch.

After welcoming the women, I whispered to Dad that he should take Mom on to lunch.

"All right. We'll bring you back something." He kissed my cheek.

"I love him," Max said. "Her, not so much."

Shaking my head slightly, I approached the women to see if they needed any help.

"—poor Violet," one was saying. "She used to be so involved with the Society, and I felt like it went downhill after she left."

"Why did she leave again?" the other woman asked. "I've forgotten."

"She had a falling out with the Greenfields."

"I couldn't help but overhear your mention of the Society," I said. "Did you mean the Southern Appalachian Renaissance Society?"

"Yes." The one who'd mentioned the Society looked affronted at my asking about it. "Why?"

"I've been making costumes for some of the members, and I'm planning to add some to my prêt-a-porter line as well."

She brightened. "Oh, how nice. Thank you for letting us know."

"Anytime." I left the women to browse in peace, but I made a mental note to ask Thomas Wortley if he knew anything about an argument between Ms. Cross and the Greenfields.

Chapter Twelve

Before Mom and Dad returned from lunch, I got a call from Cassie. When I saw her name on the screen, I dreaded answering.

"Hi, Cassie. Is he at it again?"

"No," she said. "Actually, he's been behaving himself since this morning, so thanks for that. I'm calling to let you know I ordered a coconut cream pie and a strawberry pie from Anthony's Desserts. I'll pick them up after work. Then should I come to you?"

"It depends." I winced as I asked the question. "Would you ask him a question for me?"

"Who? Anthony?"

"No...our friend with the typewriter."

"No way," Cassie said.

"I'll come to you then. I have a question for him."

Mom and Dad came through the atelier door. Dad held up a white bakery bag.

"My mom and dad are here with my lunch, Cassie. I'll see you after work." When I ended the call, I asked, "Did you two have a pleasant lunch?"

"It was delicious." Dad handed me the bag. "Guess what we got you?"

"Where are we going after you finish up work today?" Mom asked.

"My friend Cassie and I are going to see Jack Cross, the son of the woman who was murdered in her antique shop." I shrugged. "You're welcome to join me. Dad, is it a cookie?"

He scoffed. "I wouldn't bring you a cookie for lunch. I mean, I might've had I thought about it, but it would have been in addition to this chicken salad croissant."

"That sounds yummy. Thank you." I sat down behind my desk and took my wrapped croissant from the bag. After spreading out a napkin, I opened the sandwich. "I didn't realize how hungry I was."

"Did you know that woman well?" Mom asked.

"What woman?" I knew it wouldn't be that easy to divert her attention but, hey, I tried.

"The woman who owned the antique shop," Mom said. "You must have known her well if you're going to visit her son."

"Cassie knew her better than I did. They were close," I said. "But I did visit Ms. Cross's shop fairly often. In fact, Zoe and I stopped in there on the day Ms. Cross was murdered. I bought some buttons and a gorgeous needlepoint portrait. It's currently at the dry cleaner's."

"Couldn't you send the son a card or something?" she asked. "We're only going to be here in Abingdon for a few days."

"I promise I won't be long. Don't you have some friends you'd like to have dinner with and catch up while you're in town?" I took a bite of the croissant. "This is good. Thanks for bringing it."

"We came to town to visit our daughter, not make small talk with people we haven't seen in years," Mom said.

"I'll go over to the kitchen and get you a drink, Princess," Dad said. "Will a diet soda work?"

"I'd prefer a bottle of water please," I said. "Thank you."

"Anytime."

I turned back to Mom. "I won't be long, and then we'll have all evening together." Before taking another bite of my croissant, I decided to try drawing Mom into a conversation about Renaissance costumes. "This festival is apparently going to be a big deal. I'm planning to make some costumes for my prêt-a-porter line in addition to the custom ones."

"I'm not sure that's feasible," she said.

I pretended to consider her suggestion while I nibbled my sandwich. Of course, it was feasible. "I could make three or four simple gowns in a couple of the more popular sizes and see how they sell."

Dad returned with my water. "Sure. If they don't sell for this Renaissance festival, they might be a hit at Halloween."

"That's true," I said. "I had a Renaissance gown that sold the day before Halloween last year. I should probably make a pirate outfit or two as well."

"His and hers," Dad said.

Mom sighed. "I worry that running a dress shop isn't a stable endeavor. Consumers are fickle—they love you one day and tire of you the next."

"If and when my business dries up, I'll pursue other avenues. For now, I'm happy with my career, and it's sustaining me financially."

"But wouldn't it be better to have a more secure position with benefits? One at a prominent company?" she asked.

"Not to me. And I have benefits—health insurance, car insurance, a retirement account." I grinned. "My employer provides for me well. Plus, I'd rather be in charge of my own company than be employed at someone else's whim."

"That's because you've always been too hardheaded to conform to authority," Mom said. "And your father and grandfather overindulged you as a child." She sniffed. "They still do, as far as I'm concerned."

Turning to Dad, I said, "And I appreciate it ever so much, sir."

He winked. "You're quite welcome."

The two of us laughed. Mom did not.

As much as I hated to admit it, I was relieved when Mom and Dad left shortly after I ate my lunch. I wouldn't have minded Dad staying, and I know he'd have enjoyed talking with Max more, but I needed to work and felt I couldn't do so adequately with Mom breathing down my neck.

Max joined Jazzy and me in the atelier. Both of them lay across the table as I sketched the male pirate outfit I'd mentioned earlier. While I didn't get many men coming to browse in my shop, some woman would love the costume for her husband. And some women might even prefer this version to the female pirate outfit.

"Give him a bright red sash," Max directed.

I did as she instructed, and it looked great.

"Now, there's a swashbuckler." She grinned.

"Hello!" Dwight called as he came through the reception room door.

"Oh, by the way, Dwight and Zoe are dropping in," Max said.

"Thanks for letting me know ahead of time," I said.

"Oooh, I like that." Zoe nodded toward the pirate costume as she put some bags on the worktable. "Look at what all I got at the craft store."

She had wire, tulle, silk flowers, brown felt, black felt, cabochons, and feathers.

Max sat up to get a closer look at everything. "I can hardly wait to see what wonderful things you come up with."

"Same here," I said.

"Thanks. I'm going to start on the circlets tonight or tomorrow," Zoe said. "I want to watch the tutorial one more time to make sure I have it."

"Maybe I can help," Dwight said. "I'll give it a go, and if I can't make anything, I'll be the model."

"I apologize for changing the subject," I said, "but this morning, I overheard two visitors to the shop talking about Violet Cross having a falling out with the Greenfields."

"The sweet weirdos who're getting the Macbeth costumes?" Zoe asked.

"The sweet eccentrics," I said. "And yes. I'm going to go by the antique store and talk with Thomas Wortley to see if he knows what the argument was about."

Max and Zoe helped me fill Dwight in on my communications with Thomas Wortley via typewriter.

"That's fascinating," Dwight said. "I'd enjoy talking with Thomas Wortley sometime."

"Maybe I can arrange for you to have the pleasure soon," I said, feeling Dad and Grandpa would like to talk with the ghost as well. Again, I considered buying the typewriter and bringing it here. Then we could all converse with Thomas Wortley until our hearts were content.

When I arrived at Abingdon Gifting Co. that afternoon, I borrowed Cassie's key and presented my solution to Thomas Wortley.

"Cassie and I are going to see Jack Cross," I said. "I'm going to ask him if I can buy this typewriter so I can—"

No.

"No? What do you mean no?"

No. I cannot leave this building.

"But I thought you were...you know...inside the typewriter."

What rubbish! Of course, I am not inside this blasted device. I am merely using it as a vehicle by which to communicate with you.

"Why don't you simply talk with me?"

You don't believe I would if I could?

"I guess. But I don't understand why you can't. My friend, Max, is a ghost, and we talk all the time.

In fact, I could video chat with her now, and she could talk with you."

No, thank you, unless she has information on capturing Violet's killer and bringing the rogue to justice.

"About that. There were two women in my shop today who were talking about Ms. Cross having a falling out with Selma and Stuart Greenfield of the Southern Appalachian Renaissance Society. Do you know anything about an argument between Ms. Cross and the Greenfields?"

For a moment, there was no activity. Then he wrote:

Those scoundrels accused Violet of embezzling money from their so-called Society. Violet was the most morally upright person I have ever known. I would venture to guess they were the embezzlers.

"Did they ever visit this shop?"

Not to my knowledge, although they might have visited her in her home upstairs.

"You didn't go upstairs?"

Certainly not. That was Violet's private dwelling, and I never imposed upon her there.

"I'll see what I can learn from Jack. Did he and his mother have a good relationship?"

He treated her well, but there was a look about him that I did not like.

"All right. Wish me luck."

Clean paper please.

"Of course." I ripped the paper containing his words from the barrel of the typewriter and put it into my purse before inserting a fresh sheet of paper.

At least, he was saying *please* now. Well, not actually saying... Why in the world couldn't this ghost talk?

Chapter Thirteen

J ack Cross lived in a pastoral section of Abingdon. With Cassie carrying one pie and me holding the other, we walked up the steep driveway to the marble porch.

"I'd bet this place is slick in the winter," I murmured.

"The driveway or the porch?" Cassie asked.

"Both."

She rang the bell, sending a chime throughout the house.

A thin brunette with graying brown hair opened the door and greeted us with a bright smile. "Hello, Cassie. This is a nice surprise."

Cassie introduced me to Wilma Cross and told her we were there to express our condolences.

"And you've brought pie. How thoughtful." Wilma stepped back and invited us into her home. "I'll get the coffee and tea going. Jack, we have company!"

Jack was short and plump, and he had a considerable amount of energy. I couldn't help but wonder if maybe the doctor had prescribed something to help keep his spirits up during this stressful time. Or maybe he drank energy shots.

Giving Cassie a brief hug, he said, "Thank you both for coming. Go ahead and have a seat in the den, and Wilma and I will be there in a jiffy."

Jack and Wilma took the pies we'd brought into the kitchen, and I followed Cassie into the cozy den. She and I sat on the sofa.

"They seem nice," I whispered. "Is he always so wired?"

She nodded.

Wilma soon returned with a coffee and tea tray, and Jack followed with a platter of dessert plates upon which were small slices of both the coconut cream and the strawberry pie.

"We didn't know which flavor pie you'd prefer." Wilma placed her tray on the coffee table in front of the sofa. "We made it easy and gave you one of each."

"That works for me," Cassie said.

"Me too." I smiled. "You two seem like pros. Have you ever done any catering?"

"My parents owned a restaurant when I was growing up," Wilma said. "I've had plenty of practice at serving food."

Jack jabbed a thumb in Wilma's direction. "The family owned a restaurant, they all love to eat, and they're all as thin as this one. Go figure."

After serving coffee to Cassie and Jack and tea to me and herself, Wilma sat on one of the easy chairs on the other side of the coffee table. We each took a dessert plate from Jack's platter as well.

"We are both so very sorry for your loss," I said. "My assistant, Zoe, and I were in Ms. Cross's shop on Saturday afternoon. She was such a dynamo."

"That's for sure." Jack leaned back in his chair. "You don't know how many times a day I start to pick up the phone to call and check on her only to remember she's...she's not there."

"These pies are wonderful," Wilma said. "Thank you again for bringing them."

"Yes, we're grateful for your kindness," Jack said. "Everyone has been wonderful. I love that our little community rallies around each other the way it does."

"So do I." Cassie sipped her coffee. "Will you continue to operate the antique store?"

"Why? Are you interested in leasing it?" Jack leaned forward. "You could possibly talk with the owner about breaking down the wall between the two shops so you could simply expand yours. Wouldn't that be great?"

"And don't forget there's an apartment above the shop," Wilma added. "You could sublet that and make the extra money you'd need to lease the additional retail space."

"That's a fine idea," Jack said.

"Oh, no." Cassie shook her head. "I mean, it's a tempting offer, but I have plenty of space. I simply hoped you'd still be my neighbors."

"Amanda, what about you?" Wilma said. "Wouldn't you like to own the space beside your friend? It's a fantastic location."

"It certainly is," I said. "But I have a long-term agreement with Shops on Main." My agreement wasn't so much with Shops on Main as it was with

Max—I planned to be there as long as she was—but I didn't need to go down that road with the Crosses.

"Please let us know if you hear of anyone who might be interested," Jack said. "We'll make someone a generous offer on the shop's inventory and on Mother's furniture in the apartment upstairs too."

"I'll mention it to my grandpa," I said.

"Would he like to see the apartment?" Wilma asked. "Is tomorrow good for him?"

"I'll check and will let you know."

Jack quickly hopped off his chair, got a sheet of note paper and a pen, and wrote down their landline and both cell numbers.

"Thank you." I put the paper in my purse, feeling a twinge of guilt that Grandpa wouldn't actually be interested in the property. He might, however, know of someone who would be—and he could check out the place and speak with Thomas Wortley too. Grandpa might see something I'd missed.

Jason called me as I was driving home. "Hello, beautiful!"

"Hey, there, handsome. Have you had a rough day dealing with gorgeous bridesmaids and whatnot?" I was teasing, of course, but there was a little insecurity behind the remark. After all, the video Mom had found was fresh in my mind. I *did* trust Jason, but that seed Mom had planted was trying to take root.

"I wish. Today was spent doing family portraits and engagement photos. I have baby spit-up on my shirt; and with the last couple I shot, the guy was much better looking than his bride-to-be."

"Jason!"

He laughed. "I'm sorry, but it's true. How did you spend your day?"

"Um...let's see. Mom doesn't think that running a dress shop is a sustainable business, and I'm fairly certain she thinks my designing pirate costumes for next month's Renaissance festival is a waste of time."

"A Renaissance festival? Cool! Why haven't I heard about that?"

"I don't know," I said. "I hadn't heard about it either until Stuart and Selma Greenfield came in and asked me to make their Macbeth costumes. The festival is being held in Brea Ridge."

"Huh. I wish I'd known about it sooner. I could've probably done some photo packages for the attendees."

"I'll get you the Greenfields' contact information. You might still be able to do something with them—if you don't have weddings lined up the whole time the festival is happening."

"Thanks."

I considered telling him—in a joking way, of course—about the video Mom found, but I decided not to go there. I trusted Jason, and I didn't want to create conflict and doubt between us when we were having to spend so much time apart.

When I got home, Dad was lounging on the sofa watching television. Jazzy was asleep on his lap.

"Hey, there." Dad gave me a lazy wave. "I kinda like this cat of yours."

"The feeling is obviously mutual."

Mom came into the room. "I put your dinner in the fridge if you'd like to heat it up."

"Great, thanks."

Knowing Mom would only tell me something about beggars not being choosy if I asked what dinner was, I merely went into the kitchen, opened the fridge, and took out a pot with a foil-covered top. I removed the foil, found that the pot contained spaghetti, and I placed it on the stove to warm.

Mom joined me in the kitchen and sat at the table. "How did your visit go? I didn't think you were going to be so long."

"I hadn't expected to be this late either. Both Jack and Wilma Cross tried to talk Cassie and me into taking over Ms. Cross's lease." I took a wooden spoon from the drawer and stirred the spaghetti. "There hasn't even been a funeral service for Ms. Cross yet. Why would they be so eager to sell off the inventory and sign over the lease?"

"Maybe they're in financial trouble," she said. "It could also be that Ms. Cross didn't have life insurance. If she didn't, the family might now be in a bind wondering how they're going to pay for everything. It's hard for some families to even grieve properly when they're worried about giving their loved one a proper burial."

A life insurance policy.... Could that have been what Jack was searching for in his mother's shop?

"I hadn't even thought of that, Mom."

"Your Dad and I saw a situation like that firsthand in Florida. Our neighbors had to take a second mortgage out on their home to pay for the husband's mother's funeral and burial plot."

"Funerals are that expensive?" I spooned some of the spaghetti onto a plate.

"They are. But don't worry. Your dad and I have more than adequate life insurance coverage."

"Hush! I can't stand to think about anything happening to you or Dad!"

"*You* can't stand it? How do you think *we* feel?"

As she and I were both laughing, Dad came into the kitchen.

"What's so funny?" he asked.

"Never mind," Mom said. "Are the playing cards still in the drawer beneath the microwave, Mandy?"

"As far as I know."

"David, get the cards and let's play some rummy."

I went to bed after a fun evening of playing cards with Mom and Dad. He trounced us, so Mom and I accused him of cheating. He called us sore losers. This was the type of evening I'd missed spending with my parents.

I felt as if I'd barely closed my eyes when my phone rang. I came fully awake and sat up in the bed. It was four in the morning, and the screen announced the caller was Trish Oakes.

A bead of sweat snaked down my spine as I answered the call. "Ms. Oakes? What's wrong?"

"There's been a break-in, Amanda. Is there any way you can come on down to Shops on Main?"

"I'll be right there."

Chapter Fourteen

It was only four a.m., so I didn't wake Mom and Dad. I didn't want to worry them when I didn't even know what had happened yet, so I'd pulled on jeans and a sweatshirt and hurried out the door as quietly as possible.

Ms. Oakes, Ford, and a pair of uniformed deputies were at Shops on Main when I got there. Jason arrived soon after.

"As you're already aware, the thieves tripped the alarm at 2:45 a.m.," Ms. Oakes was telling the officers. "They did so by entering through the front door. Even though they had to know you were on your way, they still broke into Amanda's shop."

I gasped and tried to make a beeline for my shop.

One of the deputies barred my way. "I'm sorry, but our crime scene investigator is still working in the room. You may go in when she's finished."

"If it's any consolation," Ms. Oakes said, "I peeped in before the police got here, and everything looks fine to me."

"Thank you." It was some consolation. Surely, Ms. Oakes would tell me if the fabric had been ripped up and the beautiful shelf Grandpa Dave had made for me was smashed.

"Everything's fine," Max whispered to me softly. "I've scoured both rooms from top to bottom. Nothing has been taken or disturbed."

I released a relieved breath. "Thank you."

Jason hugged me. From everyone else's perspective, I'd just thanked Ms. Oakes twice for telling me everything looked fine. Truly, though, even with Max's assurances, I still wanted to see the shop for myself.

"Did they say anything?" I asked Max.

"I'm not sure, and I don't know if the surveillance camera would catch it if they did," Ms. Oakes said.

"We'll check," one of the officers said.

"They were looking for your needlepoint portrait," Max said.

I stepped away from Jason. "I'll be right back." I hurried to the ladies' room, giving Max a slight nod to follow me. When Max joined me, I turned on the faucet to drown out the sound of my voice. "Are you sure they were looking for the needlepoint?"

"Positive. They were steamed up when they couldn't find it. One was lily-livered and threatened to leave the other behind."

"How many were there?" I asked.

"Three—two in here and one in the car. The two in here wore those knit hoods over their faces so only their eyes were showing," she said. "As far as I could tell, the one in the car wasn't wearing a mask, but I couldn't see him well. Besides, I was interested in what the two in your shop were doing."

"And they didn't take anything?"

"Not a single thing."

I frowned. "They didn't tear my place all to pieces?"

"Nope. The scared one didn't take the time. They looked around as quickly as they could, then the chicken said—and I quote: 'It's not here. She wouldn't have known to hide it. Let's get outta here before the cops show up. I'm not going to jail over a stupid needlepoint picture.'"

"I'd better get back out there. Thanks, Max."

"Anytime, darling. I'll talk with you when there are fewer people around."

I turned off the water and left the bathroom. Max returned with me to the hallway where the small group was still gathered, but she didn't say anything.

"Where's everyone else?" I asked.

"When I told them their shops were undisturbed, they decided to stay home until the investigation is concluded," Ms. Oakes said. "I'm sure they didn't want to be in the way."

"I had to check and see that everything was all right for myself," Ford said. "I'm kinda neurotic that way."

"And I came for you," Jason told me.

Smiling slightly, I slid my hand into his.

"Trish, you can probably hire Amanda's granddad to fix the doors," Ford said.

She brightened. "That's a wonderful idea. I'll call him as soon as it's a more reasonable time."

"He typically gets up around six a.m.," I told her. "And I'm sure he'll be happy to come on in and get started on the doors even if he has to move something else around. This is an emergency."

The crime scene technician came out and spoke with one of the officers, who then turned to me.

"Ms. Tucker, you may look through your shop now to see if anything is missing."

Jason and Max accompanied me into the shop. I slowly walked through the reception area, glad to see that the furniture looked all right. Max's tablet was still in plain sight on the desk.

"I'm surprised they didn't take that," I said.

"I'd have had a fit if they'd tried." Max clenched her fists.

I didn't point out that they wouldn't have known if she'd thrown the biggest fit in the world, except maybe if she'd turned the tablet on—and then they'd have likely thought it was a glitch.

"They probably thought it wasn't worth much," Jason said.

"It's worth a bushel to me, mister!" Max said.

Not responding to either of them, I wandered slowly through the reception area and into the atelier. My laptop was charging on the worktable.

"Did they turn any lights on—you think?" I asked.

"No," Max said. "They used flashlights."

"I doubt it," Jason said. "Of course, they'd already triggered the alarm, so they might have." He sighed. "Maybe they didn't realize they'd set off the alarm until they broke into your shop. Then they ran."

"That's probably it." I looked around the work-room. "I'm relieved everything is all right."

"So am I." He put his hands on my shoulders. "Why don't you let me drive you home? Since your parents are in town, one of them can bring you in later if you're feeling up to it."

"She'll absolutely be feeling up to it," Max said. "She's not about to let some two-bit thieves run her out of her shop."

"Right." I went back into the hallway where Ms. Oakes and the officers stood. "I don't believe any-thing is missing. Jason is going to drive me home, but I'll be in at my usual time."

"All right," Ms. Oakes said.

One of the officers handed me a card. "Call us if you later determine that there is something missing or if you recall anyone acting suspiciously in or around your shop lately."

I promised I'd do so and then allowed Jason to lead me out to his SUV.

"Don't worry," he said. "All my camera equipment is in the back. You won't have to move anything out of your way."

He was right. The black leather seats—both front and back—looked as if the vehicle had been driven off the showroom floor mere days, rather than years, before. The windows, on the other hand, bore testament to Rascal's nose and tongue.

By the time Jason and I arrived at my house, it was nearly six a.m. There was a light on in the kitchen, and I invited Jason inside.

"Are you sure your parents won't mind?" he asked.

"They might." I shrugged. "Let's go find out."

When I opened the door, Dad came into the living room with a mixing bowl and spoon in his hand. "Where have you been?"

"Ms. Oakes called me. There was a break-in at Shops on Main." I rubbed the back of my neck. "The thieves set off the alarm when they came through the front door, but they still smashed my lock and went inside Designs on You."

Dad jerked his head toward the kitchen. "You two come on in here and sit down. I'm making breakfast."

We followed Dad and sat down at the table while he added a teaspoon of vanilla extract to the bowl.

"Pancakes?" I asked.

"You know it," he said. "Jason, you're being awfully quiet. Did they break into your shop too?"

"No, sir. I only went to make sure Amanda was all right."

"That was good of you," Dad said. "I appreciate that. Did they take anything from your shop?"

"I don't think so, but the officer told me to let them know if I find that anything is missing." I stifled a yawn. "I won't be able to take Jazzy into work with me until the doors are fixed, though. That stinks...and I dread telling Mom."

"Mom just heard." She came into the kitchen and peered over Dad's shoulder to see what he was making. Turning back to me, she asked, "Do you still think being self-employed beats working somewhere safer and more secure?"

"I do. Mom, this is Jason Logan. Jason, Terri Tucker."

They exchanged nice-to-meet-yous before Mom asked, "How did you know about the break-in, Jason, when we're only learning about it now?"

"Ms. Oakes called all the vendors," he said. "Only Ford and I came to the building—"

"Ford!" Dad whirled around with a look of horror on his face. "My Hemingway!"

I smiled. "Antiquated Editions was untouched, Dad."

"Are you sure? I'm calling Ford as soon as we eat breakfast...and I'm getting that book today."

"Jason, how do you like your eggs?" Mom asked. "I've been wanting the four of us to sit down and have a meal together, and I guess this is as good a time as any."

Mom decided to stay home so Jazzy wouldn't feel deserted. At least, that's what she *said.* I was guessing she was still tired from traveling on Monday and was readjusting to being here in Abingdon. Dad drove me to work so he could get his book, and I suggested we check with Grandpa Dave to see if Ms. Oakes had hired him to fix the doors.

"If she has, I'll be happy to help him," Dad said.

"Before we get there, you should know Max told me the thieves were looking for the needlepoint I bought at Ms. Cross's shop."

"That means the same people who killed Violet Cross likely broke into your place. I'm taking you back home."

"No, you aren't," I said. "At work is the safest place I can be today."

"You're right. What about your mother being at the house?"

My mind raced. There was no way the thieves could know where I lived—right? But how had they known where my shop was? That I was the one who'd bought the needlepoint? That I owned Designs on You? That I'd taken the needlepoint to my shop and not to my home?

"I have to talk to Thomas Wortley," I said.

"The ghost? Who lives in the typewriter?"

"He doesn't live in the typewriter—he only uses it to communicate. For some reason, he can't talk." I frowned. "I'm not sure if it's a physical thing—that he was mute when he died—or that he simply can't talk beyond the grave or something. Max must be pretty advanced."

"Yes, I can imagine Max would be ahead of her time no matter what," he said.

"I did tell Mr. Cross last night that I'd try to set up a meeting for Grandpa to look at Cross's Antiques. Do you think the two of you could go check out the shop and see if you happen to find anything I've missed?"

"And talk with the ghost?"

I inclined my head. "Well, yeah. But if Trish Oakes has got Grandpa working on the broken door frames, I might have to ask Zoe and Dwight to do that sooner because I need some answers."

Chapter Fifteen

Grandpa Dave's truck was in the parking lot when Dad and I got to Shops on Main.

"I suppose that answers our question," Dad said. "Ms. Oakes has him fixing the doors."

Since we didn't see Grandpa when we went inside, I guessed he was upstairs talking with Ms. Oakes.

Connie hurried out of Delightful Home and gave me a hug. "I'm sorry about the break-in, but I'm so glad the thieves weren't able to make off with any of your merchandise. I can't imagine why they'd go ahead and smash through your door after they'd already set off the alarm."

Ella and Frank joined us in the hallway.

"Last night's break-in proves that what happened to Violet Cross wasn't an isolated incident," Ella said. "I'm going to call the police and find out what measures they're taking to protect us small business owners."

"In the meantime, I'll be manning my post here in the hall." Frank jerked his head toward the card table.

"Thank goodness no one was here when the thieves broke in," Dad said.

"Amen to that." Frank grimaced. "They might've had guns or something."

We heard footsteps on the stairs and turned to see Grandpa and Trish Oakes followed by Ford.

"Dave, I'll be happy to help you fix the door frames," Ford said.

"I can lend my assistance to that task," Dad said, "I need you to guard that Hemingway until I can get up there to buy it."

"I promise you that book is safely locked away and waiting for you."

Grandpa came and kissed my cheek. "You all right, Pup?"

"I'm fine." I gave him a hug. "I'm glad you're fixing the doors." I knew with him doing the work, it would be done right.

"This job shouldn't take too long." Grandpa turned to Dad. "I'll welcome your help, but it isn't necessary if you have something else you need to be doing."

"I'm looking forward to it," Dad said. "It'll feel like old times."

"Where's Terri?" Grandpa asked.

"She's home with Jazzy," I said. "I'm going to call and check in with her." I looked at my colleagues. "Thanks for your support. You're all the best."

I went into the atelier, fished my phone from my purse, and called Mom.

"Do you miss me already, or don't you trust me with your cat?" she asked, in lieu of answering with a normal greeting.

"Neither," I said. "I just wanted you to be safe while Dad is here with Grandpa making repairs. Keep the doors locked please."

"I will." Her voice changed. "Are you scared, honey? Do you want me to come to the shop?"

"No, I just..." I couldn't tell her the truth—that my friend the ghost told me the thieves had been after something I bought at Cross's Antiques on Saturday. "This whole thing has me on edge, and I want you to take precautions today. Humor me, all right?"

"Yeah, sure. And call me if you need me."

"I will," I said. "Maybe after Grandpa and Dad get done, the four of us can grab lunch somewhere—or if that doesn't work, we can get dinner."

"That sounds nice. I enjoyed talking with Jason this morning. He's charming..."

I could tell there was the inevitable *but* coming.

"But I still don't trust him," she said. "That video made me suspicious. The bridesmaid who wrote her number on his hand was awfully pretty. I'm not saying you're not attractive too, but he might simply want to have his cake and eat it too."

"I do trust him, Mom. Yes, he's gorgeous and friendly, and it's only natural that girls are going to flirt with him. That doesn't mean he's going to cheat."

"I'd keep an eye on him anyway if I were you. It doesn't pay to go through life with blinders on."

"Duly noted," I said. "I'll talk with you later."

After ending the call, I noticed Max sitting in front of my laptop.

"Hi. Did you hear the whole thing?"

"Of course." She clicked a button, and the song *Suspicious Minds* by Elvis Presley began to play.

I laughed. "Yep. That could be Mom's theme song."

She turned it off. "Dwight and Zoe will be here soon. I believe Dwight wants to see if Dave needs his help on the doors. I know he doesn't, but I imagine Dwight is pretty handy—Daddy always was, and I'd expect he'd have taught his grandson a few things."

"I actually have another task I'd like Dwight and Zoe to handle for me," I said.

"What is it?"

I turn to see Zoe walking into the atelier from the reception area.

"Hi." I smiled at her. "Where's your papaw?"

"He's out front with your dad and Dave. What's up?"

"I can't leave, so I'd like for the two of you to go to Cassie's shop—remember, we were going to ask her to watch Jazzy for us while we went into the antique store on Saturday?"

"Yeah," Zoe said. "But the ferrets were going berserk, so we took Jazzy with us. What do you need us to go there for?"

"If you're willing—and if you don't want to, I'll find a way to—"

"Just tell me," she interrupted.

"I believe she wants you to go talk with Thomas Wortley," Max said. "Isn't that exciting? You could video connect us so we could all talk to him."

"You don't have to do it," I said.

"No, I want to." She looked from me to Max and back again. "I mean, you've said he's nice. Right?"

"He is. And I have some important questions for him."

"Yeah, Aunt Max told us about the thieves wanting your creepy old needlepoint thing." She shuddered. "I told you something was off with that picture. Ugh...somebody stabbed that image of a kid's face a bazillion times."

Max laughed. "I never thought about it like that."

"I'll get Papaw, and we'll head over to Cassie's place for the key," she said.

Within half an hour, Max and I were sitting at the laptop in the workroom video chatting with Zoe and Dwight. I hoped we were about to add Thomas Wortley to the conversation.

"Thomas, can you hear me?" I asked.

The keys on the typewriter wrote: *yes.*

"That's amazing!" Dwight said. "How do you do that? I mean, I know how you're doing it, but it's just incredible."

Nothing. But then I'd already realized Thomas wasn't much for small talk.

"There was a break-in at my shop last night," I said. "Max, the woman sitting to my right, heard the thieves say they were looking for the needlepoint I bought there on Saturday. Do you know why anyone would want that needlepoint?"

It was the one of the child?

"Yes."

I do not know what would make that particular portrait special.

"Could that be what Jack was searching for in the shop?" I asked. "Or could he have been searching for his mother's will? When we visited Jack and his wife last night, they both seemed eager to sell the inventory and get someone to take over the lease as soon as possible."

You are asking too many questions at once.

Dwight laughed. "That is simply fantastic!" He waved his hands. "Not as mind-blowing as talking with you, Aunt Max, but this is something else."

"I agree," she said. "Mr. Wortley, we find you to be the elephant's eyebrows."

Did that woman insult me?

"She didn't," I said. "We're all agreeing that you're wonderful."

Someone wonderful would have been able to protect Violet. He would have at least been able to convey who did the deed in order to bring her killer to justice.

"Cool. You talk kinda like Batman," Zoe said.

You—Amanda Tucker—ask me your questions one at a time.

"Did Violet ever indicate she was having financial difficulties?" I asked.

Violet was not having financial difficulties.

"Are her son and his wife experiencing financial trouble?"

Violet speculated, but she knew nothing for certain.

"What about her life insurance policy?" Max asked. "Sorry, but we're trying to figure out why the Crosses seem to need money. Is it to give his mom a proper send-off?"

"Did Violet have a life insurance policy that you are aware of?" I asked Thomas Wortley.

I do not know. She kept all her private documents upstairs.

"Did Jack know that? You told me he'd been searching the shop."

Violet loved her son. I would imagine she told him were her important documents were kept. She realized she was growing older.

"And you could soon be together?" Max asked.

Yes.

"That's so romantic!" She fanned her face with both hands. "I might cry."

There was a banging on the antique shop door. Someone over a loudspeaker said, "Open up! This is the police!"

Chapter Sixteen

Zoe stared at her phone—or, rather, us—wide-eyed. "What do we do?"

"Quick—take the paper from the typewriter and put it in your pocket," I said.

"Then stay mum," Max added. "Your papaw can handle the coppers."

Dwight went to open the door. Although we couldn't see them, we could hear the exchange between him and the police.

"Hello!" Dwight greeted them as brightly as if he'd invited the officers over for coffee and was delighted to see them. "Please come in."

"Sir, how did you get into this store?"

Zoe eased the paper from the typewriter and folded it behind her back. The phone was moving erratically as she did so.

"Gee whiz, kiddo, hurry," Max said. "You're making us dizzy."

After sliding the paper into the back pocket of her shorts, Zoe stepped forward.

"With this key," Dwight was saying.

Max and I couldn't see anything at this point except the ceiling, but we could still hear.

"And how did you come by a key to Violet Cross's shop?"

"Who was that?" Max asked. "He sounded too old to be a copper."

Dwight might've heard her. Either way, he asked, "Who are you, sir?"

"Helbert Justice. I own the hardware store next door."

"Well, what are you doing here?" Dwight asked.

"I'm here to see what you're doing here!" The man was practically sputtering in his anger.

"Mr. Justice, let us handle this please."

One of the officers, I mouthed to Max.

"Zoe, darling, can you give us a visual?" she asked. "If nothing else, say you're chatting with your boss

Gayle Leeson

and allowing her to see what's going on in case one of these palookas tries to rough up your papaw."

"Oh, that's good," I said softly, as Zoe turned her screen toward the action.

"Now, sir, who are you and how did you get that key?" one of the officers asked Dwight.

"I'm Dwight Hall. Violet Cross gave this key to Cassie of Abingdon Gifting Co.—also next door. My granddaughter and I were in Cassie's shop when Cassie thought she heard noises in this shop, and we came over to investigate." He looked at Mr. Justice. "Is that why you're here as well?"

"We'll ask the questions, Mr. Hall," said the officer. "Did you find the source of the noise upon entering the shop?"

"Cassie has reported hearing a tapping noise fairly often." Dwight chuckled. "Unless the shop is haunted by a ghost who enjoys typing, I imagine this place is home to a mouse or two."

Max laughed. "I knew Dot's boy would come through like a champ."

The officer nodded to his partner. "I believe we've adequately investigated this so-called noise. Let's go; and Mr. Hall, I'll need that key."

"It isn't mine to give," Dwight said. "I'll let you take possession of it and use it to lock the door if

{ 166 }

you'll promise to either return it to Cassie Rowe or else tell her that you're taking it."

"All right," the officer said. "I can do that."

Zoe clicked off the video chat as she began walking toward the door.

Closing the laptop, I turned to Max. "Now what?"

"Now we wait for them to call and give us the rumble."

"I hope they call soon." I got up and started pacing. "This entire situation makes me a wreck. If the police take Cassie's key, we won't be able to talk with Thomas anymore. And I feel like there's still so much he can tell us."

"Stay calm." She nodded toward my sketchbook. "Do something productive. Redirect your energy into creating—that's what you do best."

"You're right." I grabbed my sketchbook and pencils and sat back down at the table. "I got the male pirate costume sketched out yesterday. Let's work on the female version of the outfit."

"Give her a bodice that will enhance her assets." Max laughed. "And a flouncy skirt to hide her deficits."

Following Max's advice, I meant to make a comical dress with exaggerated assets and deficits. But when I began sketching it, I got a real feel for the dress and created a pirate costume that would flatter women of every size and shape.

Connie tapped on and then opened the atelier door. "I thought I'd see if you'd like some coffee or tea."

"No, thank you." I turned the sketchbook around to face her. "What do you think?"

"I love it." She came on into the room and closed the door behind her. "Who's it for?"

"I'm planning to make it in a couple of different colors and sizes for my ready-to-wear collection since the Renaissance Festival in Brea Ridge is coming up in a few weeks."

"That's right." She seemed surprised. "The festival is next month, isn't it? I'd forgotten all about it."

"Are you planning to go?"

"I'll talk with the kids and see if it's something they'd like to do. Matt and I took them to a RenFaire in Tennessee once, but they were much smaller then." She smiled. "They might enjoy it even more now that they're older."

My phone rang. I looked at the screen and saw it was Zoe. "Excuse me."

Connie waved and slipped out the door.

"Zoe, are you and Dwight okay?"

"We're fine. We're in the car heading back to the shop."

I put the call on speaker to facilitate Max's ability to participate in the conversation. "Did the police take Cassie's key?"

"No," Zoe said, "but they're going to call Jack Cross and see if he wants it returned."

"They also tried to give us some cock-and-bull about the place being a crime scene," Dwight said. "But I told them that after seeing it inside, I'm considering leasing the property."

"We figured that might buy us some time with Violet Cross's son if he's that eager to get the place off his hands," Zoe said.

"Good thinking," Max said. "I'm proud as peaches of you two for being able to think on your feet like that."

"We probably inherited that trait directly from you, Aunt Max," Zoe said.

"Well..." Max fluffed her hair. "I was rather clever in my day."

I started to tell her she was still clever, but I didn't want her head to swell any bigger than it already was.

"I just hate we had to leave poor Thomas with an empty typewriter," I said.

"Oh, we didn't," Zoe said. "After ending our chat, I dropped my class ring onto the floor. While I pretended to look for the ring I'd already palmed, Papaw came to help me."

"Once she'd shown me that she had the ring, I figured out right quick what she wanted me to do, so I put a sheet of paper in the typewriter."

Zoe laughed. "One of the cops asked Papaw what he was doing, and he said he was putting fresh paper in the typewriter for the ghost."

"I told 'em that for all we knew, it was Edgar Allan Poe." He snickered. "That was pretty good, if I do say so myself."

"That's when I popped up off the floor and said, 'Found it!' Then we left."

Max clapped. "Marvelous! The apples don't fall far from the tree in this family."

"Neither do the nuts," I said.

Since Zoe was in the shop working on circlets while Dwight and Frank were overseeing Grandpa and Dad's door reparations, I went to the dry cleaner's to pick up the needlepoint portrait. I guessed it must be really valuable to warrant the thieves breaking into the shop. And since Max told me one of the burglars said he wasn't going to go to jail over a stupid needlepoint, I also surmised that the thieves had been paid to break into my shop. Eager to determine why the portrait was so valuable, I was going to pick up the piece and take it to Monica for her professional assessment.

As I drove to the dry cleaner's, I called Cassie through my Bluetooth device.

"Hi, Amanda," she answered. "I imagine you heard about our exciting morning."

"I did. I'm sorry about all of that. Zoe, Dwight, and I were video chatting through most of it." I quickly explained to Cassie that Thomas Wortley didn't think Violet Cross was having financial problems but that Ms. Cross had believed Jack and Wilma were.

"That would explain them being so eager to get out of the lease," she said. "Frankly, though, I can't imagine the owners would really be okay with someone tearing out a wall in order to make their shop bigger."

"I can't either," I said. "Do you know Mr. Justice? He apparently owns the hardware store and is the one who called the police on Dwight and Zoe."

"I've met him a time or two. Seems pretty persnickety if you ask me."

"Did he and Ms. Cross get along?" I asked.

"I'm not sure, but I don't think they did. Violet mentioned to me on at least two occasions that Mr. Justice was too nosy and was always trying to find out her business." Cassie raised her voice. "Hello! Is there anything I can help you find today?"

"I'll let you go. Talk to you later."

"Okay," she said. "Bye."

I ended the call and drove on to the dry cleaner's. The needlepoint had been cleaned.

"What do you think of it?" I asked, as the cashier rang up the cost.

"It's lovely," she said. "Did you make this?"

"No. I bought it from Cross's Antiques. I couldn't imagine someone letting a precious heirloom—which is what I'm guessing this must be—wind up for sale in an antique shop."

She shrugged. "Whoever brought it in must not have had any sentimental attachment to it and preferred to have the few bucks they sold it for. Family members often don't treasure the knickknacks and collections their parents gathered for years."

"True. But so many hours' work went into this portrait. It made me sad to see it in Ms. Cross's shop gathering dust."

"Wasn't that a shame about Ms. Cross?" she asked. "She used to come in every other Wednesday."

"I didn't know her terribly well, but I thought she was a sweet person. I can't imagine why anyone would want to hurt her. Can you?"

The woman obviously didn't feel the needlepoint portrait was worth much, apart from sentimental value, but maybe she could provide some other clue as to why someone might have murdered Violet Cross. Although what information a dry cleaner would be privy to was beyond me. Did Ms. Cross wear white after Labor Day? Had she left a top-secret CIA file in her trench coat when she'd brought it in to be cleaned?

"No idea," the woman said.

So much for her providing any clue as to the identity of Ms. Cross's murderer. I wished the woman a good day and left. After putting the needlepoint portrait in the back of my car, I said a silent prayer that I wasn't being watched by the thieves or the person who'd hired them. If I was, they'd know I was once again in possession of the thing they wanted.

Chapter Seventeen

After dropping off my purse at Designs on You, I took the needlepoint portrait upstairs to have Monica appraise it. Although Zoe graciously stayed to see to clients—and finish the circlet she'd been making—Max was at my side as I carried the portrait up the stairs.

"Behave," I whispered.

"Pffft! Where's the fun in that?"

Hearing a man's voice before stepping into Monica's Menagerie, I tried to enter the shop as unobtrusively as possible. Monica wasn't having that.

"Amanda, hi! I'll be with you in just a moment."

"Take your time," I told her. I'd have given the middle-aged gentleman with her a friendly nod, but he didn't acknowledge that I'd entered the room.

"I want you to hold the E. C. Brewster for me until I return from the bank. Can I have your word on that?"

"You have my word, Mr. Samuels," she said, picking up the clock between them and putting it behind the counter. "See?"

"All right. I'll be back." With that, he left the shop.

"Wow." I waited until I heard Mr. Samuels' footsteps on the stairs. "He was adamant about that clock."

Monica smiled. "It's an E. C. Brewster."

I'd heard the man say that, but it didn't mean a thing to me. That fact must've registered on my face.

"It appraises for three-thousand dollars," she said. "He's getting it at a real bargain—fifteen hundred."

I blinked. The clock hadn't appeared all that impressive to me. But then, I didn't know much about clocks.

"I brought the needlepoint I asked you to appraise for me," I said.

"All right. Let me see what you've got there."

Placing the needlepoint on top of the glass case, I watched her face to gauge her reaction. She appeared to be mildly interested—nothing more, nothing less. She asked if she could remove the needlepoint canvas from the frame.

"Sure—be my guest," I said.

Monica carefully removed the portrait and turned it over to look at the back. "It doesn't appear to be especially old." She returned the canvas to the frame. "And the frame is nice, but it isn't gold leaf or anything. I'd value this at seventy-five to a hundred dollars."

"Really?"

"Sorry. But, hey, if you bought it and like it, what does it matter what it's worth in the marketplace?" She bit her lip. "You didn't pay over a hundred dollars for it, did you?"

"Oh, not even close."

She blew out a breath of relief. "Well, thank goodness for that. I mean, it *is* pretty, but it doesn't hold a great deal of monetary value."

"Thanks so much for taking the time to give me the appraisal, Monica. I really appreciate it."

"Anytime." She smiled. "Sorry it wasn't worth a million dollars."

I laughed. "Me too."

"Well, it if was, we'd know why that bunch of goons broke in here trying to get their mitts on it," Max said.

Managing to tune Max out as I carried the needlepoint back to my shop, I kept thinking I was missing something. If it wasn't the needlepoint itself that was valuable, I'd thought there must be something special about the frame—or *inside* the frame. But I'd been standing right in front of her when Monica took the back off the frame, and there was nothing hidden inside—no treasure map, no old stock certificates, no last will and testament...

Why *had* those goons broken in here trying to get their mitts on it?

"Monica doesn't know everything," Max said. "I heard what I heard. Those masked miscreants were after that portrait."

"Ugh." Zoe looked up from the wire she was bending with a small pair of pliers. "I take it Monica said the creepy needlepoint isn't worth much?"

"She said it was worth less than a Benjamin!" Max smirked. "Didn't think I knew that word, did you? I learned it online—means a hundred bucks."

"You're right, though," I told her. "Those guys broke in here for this thing, so there must be a reason. We just have to figure out what that reason is."

I cleared a space and placed the portrait on the worktable. "Look closely—maybe there's a secret message within the stitches or something."

Zoe snorted as she put her work aside and leaned over the needlepoint. "While I think that would be super cool, Veronica Mars, I don't think we're going to find—" She gasped. "Oh, my gosh! Do you see it?"

"See what?" I leaned in closer, eager to see what Zoe was looking at.

"I don't see a thing." Max rubbed her forehead. "My eyes are crossing from trying to look at all the individual stitches."

"Right there." Zoe pointed. "It says you...are...a...couple of saps." She threw back her head and laughed.

"Really? You thought that was necessary?" I asked.

"No, but it was fun."

Max blew out a breath. "I like a good gag as well as anybody, but there must be something special about this portrait. Now, what is it?"

"Is it the frame?" Zoe asked. "That's the nicest frame I've ever seen."

"Maybe so, but it isn't *gold leaf*." Max pursed her lips as if she'd been sucking on a lemon. "Miz Snooty Patootie didn't think the whole kit and kaboodle was as good as something you'd pick up from a five and dime."

After scanning the portrait and seeing nothing remarkable, I ran my hands over the frame. On the left side, I felt a slight bump. Picking up the frame, I turned it onto its right side so I could get a better look. The raised section of the frame wasn't clearly visible, but it was there—I could feel it.

"What is it?" Max asked.

"I don't know." As I spoke, I pressed in as I ran my fingers over the side of the frame. "It feels like a little—" A spring-loaded panel opened, and a computer flash drive dropped into my hand. I gasped. "This is it—this has to be what the thieves were after."

"Open it!" Zoe reached for my laptop.

Max squinted at the flash drive. "What's in that tiny container? It couldn't be anything very big. Diamonds maybe?"

"No, Aunt Max. You plug that *tiny container* called a flash drive into your computer. It has information on it."

"What kind of information?"

Handing me the laptop, Zoe said, "That's what we're getting ready to find out."

I shook my head. "I don't like the idea of opening a flash drive of unknown origin on my laptop. What if it's software that can copy and transmit my personal information to some hacker or wipe everything off my computer? Or both?"

"Hmm, I hadn't thought of that." Zoe looked down at the drive. "We could maybe open it at the library on a public computer."

"We could," I agreed, "but I'd rather do things the right way in case there's evidence of some sort of crime on this drive. I'm going to call the officer who was here this morning and tell him about it."

"Ah, nuts." Max sighed. "I was hoping the container could help us get to the bottom of why Violet Cross was killed."

"I'm pretty sure her murder has something to do with whatever is on this flash drive," I said. "And we'll know soon enough."

I'd spoken to the deputy and was waiting for him to arrive when Imelda Stanbury came into the shop.

This time, there was a young man with her. He appeared to be in his late teens, and while I wouldn't have called him handsome, he was awfully cute. By the way Zoe's eyes lit up, I think she agreed.

Max did and said as much. "I don't think he's much older than you, Zoe—just enough to make things interesting."

"Hello, Ms. Stanbury," I said.

"Please. I've already told you to call me Imelda." She swept her arm toward the young man. "And this is my grandson, Dylan."

I introduced them both to Zoe.

"What're you making?" Dylan asked Zoe.

"A circlet—it's for the Renaissance Festival." The color rose in her cheeks. I didn't know whether it was because she was embarrassed because Dylan was paying attention to her or because she was self-conscious about her work. Maybe both.

"Are you going?" he asked.

"Yeah, sure." She raised and lowered one thin shoulder.

"So is Dylan." Imelda beamed. "That's part of the reason why we're here."

"I've already told you, Grandma, I'm not wearing a costume." He rolled his eyes at Zoe.

She gave him a small smile. "I don't know. Amanda has designed some great costumes."

"The other reason we're here is because I found this charming little necklace that I thought might complement my outfit." Imelda pulled up a photo on her phone and turned it around for me to see. "What do you think of this? Isn't it cute?"

"It is," I said. "And I think it would go beautifully with your wise woman costume."

"Wonderful." She looked around the shop.

"Is there something else you're looking for?" I asked.

"Oh, well, you have such lovely outfits here," Imelda said. "Doesn't she, Dylan?"

Another eyeroll. "I guess."

"He doesn't care about outfits," Max said. "He's chatting up a pretty girl."

Zoe's blush deepened.

"Max," I chided.

"What?" Imelda asked.

"Maximize...fashion...I always say." Yikes. She probably thinks I'm doing a William Shatner impression.

Smile faltering, Imelda said, "Yes, of course. I, um, heard about your break-in."

"Really?" I asked. "It only happened a few hours ago. Surely, it hasn't made the news yet."

"No, but you know how word travels in a small town." She held up a lime green wiggle dress and perused it before hanging it back on the rack. "I hope nothing was damaged or taken."

"Fortunately, no." I smiled. "We were lucky."

"Indeed." She craned her neck looking around. I wondered if she thought she'd see bullet holes or something equally exciting.

There was a tap at the door before the officer I'd spoken with earlier started into the room.

"Hello." I hurried over to him. "Could we speak outside on the porch please?"

"All right." He moved aside so I could precede him out of the room.

"Be back in a second," I said over my shoulder.

Maybe the officer's presence would give Imelda Stanbury the excitement—or the bit of gossip—she'd been seeking.

Chapter Eighteen

Imelda and her grandson were still in the shop when I came back in after handing the flash drive over to the officer. Dylan was still talking with Zoe.

"Those two have sparked like dry kindling," Imelda said. "He'll have me here all day, if I'm not careful."

"Zoe might be the reason *he* hasn't left, but Imelda still hasn't found whatever she came here to find," Max said.

"What do you think it is?" I blamed my lack of ability to resist answering Max on a lack of sleep and agitation over the break-in.

Imelda stopped surveilling my shop long enough to jump on my question. "What do you mean, dear?"

"I wonder why any thieves would choose the targets these have—provided the same group broke into both Cross's Antiques and Shops on Main," I said. "There are businesses with more cash on hand and more valuable merchandise—to the masses, at least—than there are in an antique shop or a fashion boutique."

Overhearing our conversation, Zoe said, "Yeah, you'd think they'd try to rob a jewelry store. It'd be much easier to fence the loot."

Laughing, I said, "You've been watching too many crime shows. But you're right. Jewelry would be much easier to sell. What do you think, Imelda? What's your best guess as to why the thieves chose to break into such small, niche businesses?"

"I...I wouldn't have a clue." She looked at Dylan.

"The antique shop is easy." He leveled his gaze at his grandmother. "Antiques are valuable—some are anyway. The thieves likely thought they'd either find money or something worth selling there."

"But from what I've heard about the incident at Cross's Antiques, nothing was taken," Zoe said.

Max chuckled softly. "Watch my fiery little niece go head-to-head in a debate with a boy who obviously likes her," she whispered to me. "And vice versa."

"I'm more inclined to feel that the so-called attempted robbery of Cross's Antiques was a cover for what the burglar intended—killing Ms. Cross," Zoe continued.

"You *do* watch a lot of crime dramas, don't you?" Dylan's mouth ticked up in a half smile. "More likely, the thief or thieves were surprised by Ms. Cross, panicked, killed her, and then fled before they were caught."

"I disagree. Ms. Cross was murdered, and Shops on Main was broken into to make it seem that a gang of thieves is running around Abingdon doing smash-and-grabs at small businesses." Zoe lifted her chin.

"Or..." Dylan raised an index finger. "The thief was searching for something specific. He obviously didn't find it at Cross's Antiques, so he came looking for it here."

Bingo.

Max winced and drew in a sharp breath. "That boy is gonna blow his chance if he doesn't stop arguing with her."

"Why?" Zoe asked. "There aren't any antique shops here."

{ 187 }

"I thought Monica's Menagerie was an antique store," Dylan said.

Before the two could discuss the matter further, Imelda said, "Dylan, my blood sugar is getting low. We need to go on to lunch."

He looked at Zoe. "Would you like to join us?"

Imelda's eyes widened, and she opened her mouth to speak.

"Maybe next time," Zoe said. "I have plans today."

"That's my girl!" Max grinned. "Make him chase you."

When I was certain Dylan and Imelda were gone, I said, "They know."

"Know what, darling?" Max asked.

"I don't think Dylan was merely speculating," I said. "They know the burglars were looking for something from Cross's Antiques, and they believe I have it."

"You don't reckon Dylan was one of the thieves, do you?" Zoe asked.

I said no because of her crestfallen expression. Deep down, I wasn't so sure.

Grandpa Dave and Dad finished repairing the doors; and as their self-appointed supervisors, Frank and Dwight proclaimed it to be a job well done. Frank went back to guarding us from the hallway, and Dwight accompanied Grandpa and Dad into my shop.

"Are you about ready to go?" Dwight asked Zoe.

"Yeah." She held up the one circlet she'd completed. "What do you think?"

"I don't know." He frowned. "What is it?"

She placed it on her head.

"Well, how nice." He looked around at Grandpa. "You think I'd look good in one of those things?"

Grandpa shook his head. "It might slide off your bald head right down to your nose."

"Nah, she's got them pliers. She could tighten it up on me." Dwight grinned.

"There's a thought." Grandpa looked at Max. "You're awfully quiet today, firecracker."

She smiled. "I'm a tad whacked is all. Having robbers disturb me before daylight sapped my energy."

"Mine too," I said.

"Well, shucks," Grandpa said. "I was going to invite everybody over to my place for dinner after I go look at the antique shop this evening, but—"

"That sounds good to me." I winked at him. "You know I'm never too tired for your home- cooking."

"All right." He looked at Dad. "You think Terri would be up for it?"

"I believe so. I'll go upstairs and get my book from Ford, and then I'll go home and talk it over with her. I'll call you as soon as she gives me the go-ahead."

"How about you, Dwight?" Grandpa asked. "Are you and Zoe up for some pork chops, biscuits, and fried apples?"

"Heck, yeah, I am." Dwight looked at Zoe. "You coming with me?"

"Sure." She grinned as she packed up her materials. "Somebody has to keep you out of trouble."

"How about Maggie?" I asked.

"Um...she might have to work." Zoe didn't meet my eyes.

I knew she was likely formulating an excuse in advance in case Maggie didn't want to join us. Zoe's mom wasn't the most social woman to begin with, but she didn't particularly care for me and my friendship with her daughter.

"Have fun," Max said. "Let me know when it's going to be just us, and I'll be there with—well, *not* with bells on...just in this outfit I'm always wearing."

"Which looks gorgeous on you," Grandpa said.

"Aw, you sly old silver fox." She blew him a kiss.

Dad looked at me and spread his hands.

I shrugged. Yep, his dad was flirting with a ghost.

Later that afternoon, I was sitting at the worktable with a 2B pencil in my hand and my mind as blank as the sketchbook page I was staring at.

"Penny, darling?" Max asked.

"Hmm?"

"For your thoughts?"

"Oh," I said. "Sorry. I don't think I have any. Or, maybe, I have too many. I feel drained. Not only tired because I had to get up so early this morning but completely wiped out emotionally."

"So unlock the bag, chum. Dump everything onto the table where we can sort through it and see what we've got."

I sighed. "First of all, I think Imelda and Dylan know something about what took place at Cross's Antiques the evening Violet was murdered."

"Agreed. They at least have some idea of what the robbers were after, and they believe you have it."

"And now we know I do—or I did." I frowned. "I wonder if they know that too. If they know I bought the needlepoint, then they either believe I found the flash drive or that I'm ignorant of its existence. Maybe I should've said something about it to Imelda."

"I don't think so, darling. You don't want to invite the fox into the hen house."

"I need to know who Violet Cross told that I bought the needlepoint," I said. "Do you think someone came in asking about it after I'd left, that she kept records of who bought what, or that the thieves found her receipts and targeted everyone who was in the shop on Saturday? We don't know that other buildings or homes haven't been broken into."

"I imagine there's only one person to ask," Max said.

Nodding, I said. "She's going to hate it, but Cassie has to help us out on this one."

Chapter Nineteen

The chipper note in Cassie's voice as she greeted me when answering the phone flew right out the window when I explained what I wanted.

"Amanda, I told you I don't want anything to do with that...that..." She lowered her voice. "Ghost."

"You don't really *have* to have anything to do with him," I said. "Just unlock the door, poke your head inside, and ask Thomas if Violet kept a record of who bought what."

"That's insane. Seriously—do you realize how crazy that sounds?"

"Okay, how do you keep track of your sales?" I asked. "I mean, for me, if someone comes in and custom orders something, then I keep their names, measurements, and preferences on file. But I only keep up with the ready-to-wear items by watching the inventory."

"That's what I do. I know who buys gift baskets and for whom; but if you walk in here and buy some cheeses and bath soaps, I doubt I'll remember that. I only track the inventory, so I'll know when I need to order more of something."

"I think Violet's method must've been different from ours." I muted my line and looked at Max. "Should I tell her about the computer drive we found in the frame?"

"Absolutely not. Keep that information to yourself. We still don't know what was on that thing."

Nodding at Max as Cassie asked what I meant, I said, "I got the impression someone who came in today knew about my buying the needlepoint portrait from Cross's Antiques."

Max nodded her agreement with what I'd said.

"Why does that matter?" Cassie's voice held a hint of exasperation. Not that I could blame her—I wasn't giving her all the information.

"I'm just wondering if the thieves who broke in and murdered Violet could've seen her receipts and known if something valuable was sold within the days leading up to her death and then wondered if they could find the object."

"That's really a long shot," Cassie said.

"I know, but—" How could I get Cassie to listen to me? "—But do you want Thomas Wortley haunting us for the rest of our lives?"

"No!" She exhaled sharply. "Fine. I'll go over there, unlock the door, and yell the question to him. I'll let you know if I hear the typewriter, but I'm not going any farther into the shop than the threshold."

"That's all right. My grandpa can check the typewriter when he gets there later to look at the building with Jack."

"Whatever you say. Do you want to stay on the line with me while I go ask Typewriting Thomas your question?" she asked.

"Sure." I could hear Cassie fumbling for the keys. "Oh, shoot. Somebody's coming in. I'll take care of your pressing question as soon as I get a minute though."

"All right," I said. "Thanks."

When I ended the call, Max frowned. "Do you think she'll do it?" she asked.

"Yeah. I've never known Cassie not to keep her word."

In the meantime, I decided to get started on the muslin for Selma Greenfield's gown. Knowing I could have it ready by midday tomorrow, I called Mrs. Greenfield.

"Amanda, hello." She chuckled. "Your name came up on my screen, of course. You couldn't possibly have our costumes finished already!"

"I don't," I said, "but the fabric is scheduled to arrive today, and I'm making the muslin for your gown so you can come in for a preliminary fitting."

"What is a muslin?"

"It's kind of like a draft of your pattern. We can use the muslin to see exactly how your gown is going to fit and make any alterations before creating your actual gown. You'll be able to get a better idea of how the costume is going to look and to make any necessary changes."

"Oh, that sounds splendid," she said. "When should this muslin be ready?"

"I should have it by noon tomorrow."

"You do work quickly, don't you?" She gave another chuckle. "I like that."

"By the way, Imelda Stanbury is having me make a costume for her as well," I said.

"Really." Ms. Greenfield said it as a statement rather than a question. "What is she going to be?"

"A wise woman."

She gave a bark of laughter. "Well...what do you know?"

I let that odd remark pass without comment. "I understand that Violet Cross had also been involved with the Renaissance organization."

"At one point, yes." Her voice was stiff now.

"I simply wanted to say I'm sorry for your loss," I said. "What a blow it must've been to hear of your friend being murdered in her shop like that. It was horrifying to me, and I barely knew her from shopping with her."

"Yes, well..." She paused. "Stu and I were shocked and devastated. Poor Jack—what will he do now? Jack is her son."

"I've met him." I started to say something more about Jack or Violet but thought better of it. "So, shall I give you a call tomorrow when the muslin is ready?"

"Please do." Ms. Greenfield seemed relieved now. Whether it was because we were talking about a lighter subject than the death of Violet Cross or because she was eager to get off the phone with me, I didn't know. "I'll look forward to seeing you."

Max perched on the edge of the worktable as I ended the call. "As sure as I'm sitting here, that woman didn't give two figs about Violet Cross."

I opened my mouth and then closed it again. One could argue that Max *wasn't* physically occupying space on the worktable. But, on the other hand, I could see her sitting there. Either way, I understood the point she was making and was afraid she was right about Selma Greenfield.

Even if the Greenfields believed Violet had embezzled from them, she'd been their friend at one point and she'd been brutally murdered. How devastating that would be. Either Ms. Greenfield was an incredible actress, or she didn't give two figs about Violet Cross.

My phone rang. It was Cassie.

"Hi, there," I said.

"I did it, and he's typing even as we speak. I took care of my part—the rest is up to you."

Although I was still working when Dad and Grandpa Dave visited Cross's Antiques, I'd already given Grandpa Dave the low down—he needed to casually go over to the typewriter and remove the paper while Dad was talking with Jack Cross. Dwight had decided to wait and call Jack for an appointment to see the shop if it turned out that we had more questions for Thomas. I didn't know what Dad had told Mom he and Grandpa were doing this afternoon; but I realized that the less I said about anything in front of her, the better.

I got a call from Grandpa sooner than I was expecting to hear from him.

"Did everything go all right?" I asked. "Did you get the paper?"

"Not yet." He was talking quickly. "Jack had to go upstairs to take a phone call and will likely be back any minute. The paper is still in the typewriter, but here's what it says: *I don't know what kind of records Violet kept, but she did talk about the needlepoint portrait on Saturday after you were here. A man came in asking about it, and she said it had been bought earlier in the day.*"

"Ask him if the man was young or old," I said. "What did he look like?"

Thomas apparently heard me because the typewriter started working before I finished my questions.

"He says, *Younger. He looked like many of the ne'er do wells traipsing up and down the sidewalk in front of this building—nothing particularly remarkable about him.*" Grandpa chuckled. "I hear you, buddy."

"Does he know anything else about the guy? Had he been in before? Who brought the portrait into the shop in the first place? Maybe they—"

Clack, clack, clack, clack, clack!

"This is from Thomas, not me. *Beleaguering me about the rogue will not force me to remember anything more pertinent. Nor do I know who brought the needlepoint into the shop.*"

"Ah, Jack," I heard Dad say. "Is everything all right?"

"Yes, certainly." Jack Cross's voice was fainter, but recognizable. "Where were we?"

Grandpa Dave ended the call.

"Well, that was a bust," I said to Max.

She was sitting in front of the laptop. "Not entirely. We know now that it was a young man who went into the shop asking about the portrait."

"Yeah." I sighed. "A young man...like Dylan."

"We don't know it was Dylan. Even if it were, he must not have killed her, or Thomas would have said so."

"That's true." I began straightening up the work-table for the day. "Unless he came back and did it later that evening."

"But why would he if he knew what he'd gone in there looking for wasn't there?" Max asked. "I don't think the young man asking about the portrait is our killer."

"He might be the one who put the flash drive in the frame though."

She nodded. "Now you're on the trolley. By the way, I think I know why Thomas Wortley can't talk."

I went around the side of the table to look at the laptop screen. Max had been reading an article on Thomas Wortley's death.

Pointing to the screen, she said, "His larynx was crushed in the accident."

"Why would that matter now?" I frowned. "Your neck was broken, but it doesn't appear to be when I look at you now. Plus, you bob your head all over the place."

She shrugged. "From where I'm sitting, I think poor old Thomas is just an unlucky ghost all the way around."

Chapter Twenty

I met Dad and Grandpa Dave at Grandpa's house after work. I was going to help prepare our dinner, and Dad was going to pick up Mom after we'd discussed what had taken place at Cross's Antiques. The two men were sitting on rocking chairs on Grandpa's front porch.

"What did you two tell Mom you were doing this afternoon?" I asked, as I sat on the swing.

"Nothing," Dad said. "As far as she knows, we were still working on the doors."

"All right. I didn't want to say anything that would get any of us in trouble." Of course, saying something incendiary was never hard for me where Mom was concerned. "Did you hear anything from

Dwight or Zoe about whether or not Maggie is going to come to dinner?"

"No." Grandpa shrugged. "We'll make enough food for one more, so it won't make much of a difference either way."

Grandpa always prepared enough food that it wouldn't matter if a small army showed up, but that was beside the point. I wondered if it might make Maggie like me more or less if she met my parents.

"Tell me more about the tour of Cross's Antiques while it's only the three of us," I said.

"After I was forced to abruptly hang up from talking with you," Grandpa said, "I asked Jack if he'd mind showing me the apartment."

"I took that as my cue." Dad grinned, obviously pleased with himself for diving into the sleuthing game headfirst. "Looking at my phone, I said, 'I need to take care of this. I'll be up in a sec.' And then when the coast was clear, I replaced the paper in the typewriter."

"Great job," I said.

He spread his hands. "Eh, it was nothing." And yet he looked like a boy who'd just gained entrance into the older kids' secret clubhouse.

"Is the apartment nice?" I breathed in the fragrance of honeysuckle wafting on the breeze.

"Very," Dad said. "Her shop might've been dusty and disorganized, but Ms. Cross was an immaculate housekeeper. I told Jack—and I firmly believe it—taking over the lease is a wonderful opportunity for someone."

"Someone," Grandpa agreed, "but not me. I was never seriously considering leasing the shop anyway, and after seeing it, I realized again how good I've got it—sizeable workshop organized the way I like it, home far enough away from town to avoid much traffic and noise, no lease payment...."

I studied Grandpa. Something in the way he'd spoken made me feel that he was dwelling on something. "But?"

He shook his head. "I can't figure out why Jack would want to give the place up. He told us business was great and that his mother was doing well with it. If he wanted to hang onto the place, Jack could easily hire someone to run the business and make the apartment part of their compensation."

"We told Jack we'd think about it a little more," Dad said. "We didn't want to give him a flat-out no in case you need us to go back."

"Thanks, but I hope that won't be necessary." I told them about finding the flash drive in the needle-point frame. "Maybe the police will find something on the drive that will lead them to Violet Cross's killer. I'm ready for us to be able to close the book on the whole affair."

Dad nodded slowly. "It was kinda cool to see that typewriter working like a player piano, though. Not as incredible as talking with Max, but still..."

"Well, Pup, hadn't you and I better get dinner started?" Grandpa slapped his thighs as he stood up.

"Yes, sir, we had." I stopped the swaying swing, stood, and gave Dad a quick hug. "Would you bring Jazzy back with you? I've missed her today."

"I'll do it," he said, "despite your mother's protests."

Dad and Mom arrived with Jazzy in her carrier. Dad let the cat out, and she ran to my waiting arms. She didn't stay long, though, because she could hardly wait to greet Grandpa Dave.

"I didn't feel it was necessary to bring the cat to dinner," Mom said, "but your father insisted."

"I asked him to bring her," I said. "I didn't want her to be alone all evening. Has she been fed?"

"Not since this morning."

"Let's take care of that." Grandpa sat Jazzy onto the floor, and the two of them went into the kitchen.

"Is there anything I can help with?" Mom asked.

I wondered if she was asking because she really wanted to help or was merely being polite. Or perhaps she wanted to feel needed. I hated that everything having to do with my mother was an internal debate. With Dad, there was no drama—no looking for an ulterior motive, no power plays. We were free to be ourselves. With Mom, I wasn't sure either of us truly knew the other.

"Would you mind shucking the corn?" I was nearly finished peeling the apples, but I could easily take care of shucking the corn if Mom didn't want to do it.

"Sure." She went to the sink and washed her hands.

I washed mine again before returning to the apples. "Did you have a nice time today?"

Lifting one shoulder, she said, "It was all right. I miss being home."

"You miss living here?" I asked.

"No. I love Florida. I'm missing our home there."

"Oh." That stung. She and Dad hadn't been here but two full days, and she was already wanting to go back.

The doorbell rang, and I was glad for an excuse to leave the kitchen. When I entered the living room, Grandpa had opened the door for Zoe, Dwight, and Maggie. I was delighted Maggie had opted to join us, but I tried not to show it. I didn't want to make her feel uncomfortable.

"Hi." I addressed the group as a whole. "I'm glad you could make it."

"It sure smells good in here," Dwight said.

Maggie held out a covered pan. "I brought brownies."

"Thank you," Grandpa said.

Dad swept in and took the pan. "Somebody responsible had better take care of these."

"Give 'em to your daughter then." Grandpa winked at me.

"I'm hurt," Dad said, but he did hand me the pan.

"I'll take these to the dining room." When I turned, I saw that Mom was standing in the doorway. "Mom, have you and Dad met everybody?"

"We met Zoe and Dwight as soon as we got into town on Monday," Dad said, "but we haven't met

Zoe's mom." He held out his hand. "I'm David Tucker."

Maggie shook his hand and smiled as she looked from him to Grandpa. "That's not confusing at all."

Grandpa held up his hands in mock surrender. "Trust me—it wasn't *my* idea. It was his mother who insisted he carry on the family name."

Mom had the good sense not to point out that she hadn't actually met Zoe and Dwight because she'd been pouting on Monday; and since she blushed slightly, I thought maybe she'd regretted her earlier behavior. "I'm Terri. I won't shake your hand because mine are dirty from shucking corn. In fact, I'd better get back to it since the rest of dinner is almost ready."

About half an hour later, we were gathered around the dining room table enjoying our meal.

"I understand you were fixing some doors at Shops on Main today, Dave," Maggie said.

Zoe stiffened slightly, and Dwight mouthed *sorry* in my direction.

Trying not to smile at Dwight's clownish expression, I answered for Grandpa. "That's right. Grandpa and Dad did a terrific job on them too. You'd never know someone tried to break into the building last night. Fortunately, the alarm went off immediately, and the wannabe thieves ran away."

"Still, that must be unsettling, especially in light of what happened to Violet Cross," Maggie said.

Did Maggie subscribe to the Ella Peterman theory that there was a band of thieves targeting local small businesses?

"I was terribly sorry to hear about Ms. Violet's death," Mom said. "I used to love going into Cross's Antiques and looking at the dolls when I was a little girl." She smiled. "Some were beautiful, but others were downright creepy."

"I'll second that," Zoe said.

After taking a sip of her water, Mom resumed her recollection. "I remember asking my mother once where Ms. Violet's husband was. Mom said he'd died a few years back. Being ten or twelve and full of questions, I wondered why Ms. Violet never got another husband. She was still quite pretty then and couldn't have been more than forty-five."

Zoe and I shared a glance.

"What did she say?" I asked.

"Mom said it was because Ms. Violet was in love with Thomas Wortley, the ghost." She chuckled. "Isn't that ridiculous? But I found it heartbreakingly romantic at the time."

Chapter Twenty-One

Thursday morning, Mom and Dad followed Jazzy and me to work. I was glad they were bringing the rental car because, frankly, I hoped they wouldn't stay long. While I thought it was nice that Mom was finally showing some interest in my work, I didn't relish the idea of her breathing down my neck all day.

Once we got Jazzy settled in, I unobtrusively put a finger to my lips to keep Max from scaring Dad out of his wits.

"Nonsense," she said. "Good morning, David."

"Hey, there." He smiled. "How are you?"

"Who are you talking to?" Mom asked.

Dad merely jerked his head toward the hallway. That didn't make a lot of sense because we'd already closed the door, but she simply rolled her eyes.

"I'm fine." Max wrinkled her nose as she laughed.

That ghost was going to be the death of us all.

Sitting on a chair in front of one of the sewing machines, Mom said, "I haven't sewn in years. I'll give it a shot, though, if you need help."

"Thank you, Mom, but I'm fine."

"I believe I'll go up and take Ford a cup of coffee," Dad said.

"Good luck beating him to the kitchen," I said.

"Well...see you in a bit." He seemed relieved to have an excuse to leave. I knew he liked Max and enjoyed talking with her but not when Mom was around. And, like me, he was finding that it was easy to get distracted and forget not everyone could see and hear Max.

"I didn't realize you knew that old story about Thomas Wortley haunting the antique shop," I said to Mom after Dad had left the workroom. "Did you believe in ghosts then?"

"I might've wanted to, but that was my simply giving in to a silly, sentimental notion."

Max waved at Mom with both hands.

"Grandpa once told me that when I was a little girl, I used to claim I saw and talked with people that you and Dad couldn't see." I got out Selma Greenfield's muslin so I could finish it up.

"Sure, you had imaginary friends like most other kids, but I finally got tired of that nonsense and made you stop it." She examined her fingernails. "Please tell me you're not buying into what I said last night about Violet Cross being in love with a ghost. I only believed it because I was a child at the time. In fact, I doubt I ever genuinely believed it—I simply *wanted* to."

"Why would Granny tell you a story like that?" I asked.

She shrugged. "Who knows? Like you, Mother always had a fanciful imagination."

Having bored of my conversation with Mom, Max twirled around the room playing with Jazzy.

"I'm going to get a cup of coffee." Mom stood. "Would you like anything?"

"No, thanks. I promised Mrs. Greenfield I'd have this muslin for her to try on this afternoon, and I'd better get busy with it."

"You can't work and sip coffee at the same time?" She huffed. "What is wrong with that cat?"

I laughed as I watched Max and Jazzy play. "Maybe she sees a ghost."

Mom shook her head and went to the kitchen.

When my door opened a couple of minutes later, I didn't look up.

"You sure are absorbed in your work, sweetheart."

At the sound of Jason's voice, I stopped the sewing machine and went over to give him a kiss.

"I thought you were my mom coming back."

He kissed me again. "I'm glad she's not in here."

"Me too." For more reasons than the ability to kiss Jason privately—well, privately as far as he knew.

Mom opened the door, and I stepped out of Jason's arms.

"Good morning," she said to Jason. "No blushing brides to photograph today?"

"Not yet," he said.

From the corner of my eye, I saw Max perch atop the worktable near her tablet. Jazzy joined her and rolled from side to side, pawing the air.

"I'm getting ready to leave for Brea Ridge. I'm doing a shoot for a group of friends who graduate next spring." He smiled. "It's a group of guys who are going in different directions after high school, and they want some shots for posterity."

"I think it's cool that they're being mindful and wanting to keep a record of their time together," I said.

"So do I. It's usually girls who do the group shots." He nodded toward the reception area where there was a photo of me wearing a green 1930s evening gown hanging over the mantle. In the portrait, which he'd taken, I was standing in front of the fireplace looking back over my shoulder at him. "And then some women can't help but stand out on their own."

I could feel my cheeks burning at the compliment.

"I imagine you see lots of beautiful women during the course of your work," Mom said. "In fact, I saw a video of you with one on the internet the other day."

"Mom!"

"No, you're right, Mrs. Tucker. I see lots of pretty girls, but there none more beautiful than Amanda— at least, not in my eyes," Jason said. "I'll admit that some of the women I encounter at weddings can become flirtatious, especially after they've had a glass or two of wine. That's why I have my mom—Peggy, the Piranha, as my grandma calls her—take my calls and babysit Rascal, my dog, during peak wedding season."

There was a burst of applause from Max's tablet. I widened my eyes at Max, who had the temerity to shrug.

"How odd," Mom said.

"Jazzy..." I went over to the table, picked up the cat, and cuddled her. "What did you do?"

Dad came in then. "Wait until you see the new books that came into Ford's shop." He noticed Jason. "Oh, hi. Will you be around for dinner this evening?"

"Sorry, sir, I have a rehearsal dinner tonight," Jason said. "I do hope to be available for lunch tomorrow."

"Let us know." Dad looked at me. "Maybe you could get Zoe to come by."

"Maybe. Even if I can't, I think the shop could survive without me for an hour."

"I'll talk with you later," Jason told me. "Bye, folks."

After Jason left, Mom wandered into the reception area to look through the ready-to-wear line.

Max stepped up to Dad and asked, "Would you like to go out onto the porch for a chat?"

"Don't you have to stay here?" He immediately looked toward the reception area to see if Mom had heard his slip.

I smiled slightly and covered for him. "If I have a pressing errand or lunch with my parents who I don't get to see often, I'll leave whether Zoe can come by or not."

"I'm tethered to the *building*, darling," Max said, also answering him. "The porches are part of the building."

"Oh, okay." He walked through the reception area and told Mom, "I'm going to step out onto the porch for some fresh air."

Mom continued looking through the clothes, and Max passed through the wall to join Dad on the porch. I saw Dad take out his phone and put it up to his ear.

Smart.

Mom soon tired of being at the shop and asked Dad to take her to The Pinnacle shopping center in Bristol. I was relieved. Dad asked me to let him know if I needed anything. I told him I'd be fine.

Max disappeared, and Jazzy curled up on her bed and napped.

Deciding to enjoy the peacefulness while it lasted, I quickly finished Mrs. Greenfield's muslin and then started on her husband's pattern.

Mrs. Greenfield came into the shop alone today, eager to try on the muslin and see how her gown was going to fit.

"This entire concept of a muslin pattern is new to me," she said, as we walked behind the Oriental screen. "Don't tell anyone, but I've always bought off the rack before. I mean, I've had tailoring done, but not a lot of couture fashion." She chuckled. "Isn't it funny that my first designer gown will be turning me into Lady Macbeth?"

"It is. And you'll be a lovely Lady Macbeth." I smiled. "The fabric got here yesterday, and it's gorgeous. I'll show it to you once we've made any necessary adjustments to the muslin."

"Ooh, I can hardly wait."

The muslin gown was a little too loose in the waist, and I pinned it accordingly. The gown would also need to be shortened slightly.

"What color is Imelda's gown going to be?" Mrs. Greenfield asked.

"Cream with a red overdress." I took pins from my wrist pin cushion and tacked up the hem of her gown. "It's good you decided not to go with the emerald or else the two of you might've looked like medieval Yuletide carolers in your red and green."

She didn't find my joke amusing. "Imelda has been decidedly strange since Violet Cross's death. I can't see her attitude becoming so lighthearted as to pretend to be a caroler, even in a month's time."

"I hadn't realized Imelda and Violet Cross were close," I said. "She was in here with her grandson yesterday, and she didn't even mention Ms. Cross."

"What did you think of Dylan?" she asked.

"He was cute. I believe he and Zoe hit it off— remember Zoe, my assistant?"

"Oh, sure. Well, not to speak out of turn, but you might want to warn her about that young man."

"Really?" I frowned up at her as I finished pinning her hem. "Has Dylan been in some sort of trouble?"

"I couldn't say, but Stu and I have found him to be a tad shifty," she said. "I wouldn't want that sweet girl to get hurt."

Chapter Twenty-Two

After seeing Mrs. Greenfield, I was eager to speak with Imelda Stanbury again. I put Mr. Greenfield's muslin pattern on hold to work on the muslin for Imelda's "wise woman" gown.

And I gave her a call. "Hi, Imelda," I said when she answered. "I wanted to let you know I'll have your muslin pattern ready this afternoon for your first fitting in case you'd like to stop in before closing today or tomorrow morning."

"Oh, how exciting! I'll be there today around four o'clock. Will that work?"

"That works well." I ended the call and went to work on her muslin. Hers was a simple gown, and I knew the muslin wouldn't take more than half an hour to complete.

As I crafted the pattern, I made a mental note to go see Thomas Wortley before going home. I couldn't help but wonder—especially given the way Dylan and Imelda had behaved when they were here yesterday—if Dylan had ever been to Violet's shop or if Violet had discussed the young man with Imelda. I couldn't imagine Imelda creating a computer flash drive and hiding it in the frame, but I could see Dylan doing it.

Jason popped in as I was finishing the muslin.

I smiled. "You sure know how to brighten someone's day—twice!"

"So do you." He dropped a quick kiss on my lips. "I'm on my way back home to get ready for the rehearsal dinner, and I wanted to stop and see you."

Taking the muslin and hanging it up, I motioned for Jason to follow me into the reception area. "How was the shoot?"

"It was great. The guys are big fans of superheroes, and they posed unbuttoning their oxford shirts to reveal superhero shirts underneath. The admiration and friendship they have for each other was evident." He dropped onto one of the navy armchairs.

I sat on the other chair. "That sounds fun. I had a lot of friends in school but no one I was particularly close with—not close enough to get group photos made together prior to senior year."

"Me either," he said. "Tell me what's been going on around here while I've been out and about."

"Well, yesterday I found a secret compartment in the frame housing a needlepoint portrait I bought at Cross's Antiques on Saturday."

"Really?"

Chuckling, I said, "Absolutely. It was like something out of a spy movie."

"Was there anything inside?"

"Of course. A computer flash drive."

"Whoa." He leaned forward. "What was on the drive? Nuclear codes? A list of Russian spies? Violet Cross's grocery list?"

"I don't know."

Spreading his hands, he asked, "What do you mean you don't know?"

"I don't. I was afraid to plug it into my laptop because I didn't know if it contained a virus or something, plus I was afraid it might be what the thieves were looking for when they broke into the shop." I shrugged. "Since I bought the portrait from Violet Cross, and she was murdered that same day, I worried that whatever was on the flash drive might've been what got her killed. I turned the drive over to one of the detectives who investigated the break-in yesterday morning."

"That was actually smart thinking. I'm not so sure I could have been as restrained as you were. I'd have plugged that flash drive right into my laptop, not even considering any adverse consequences."

"Do you think the police will tell me what was on it?" I asked.

"I doubt it." He leaned back in his chair. "They'd probably tell another police officer though. I'll give Ryan a call and see if he can find anything out for us."

Jason's friend Ryan was an officer with the Winter Garden Sheriff's Department.

"Thanks. That would at least ease my mind a little...especially if it turns out to be nothing of consequence."

"In the meantime, I'm concerned about you," he said.

"Why's that?"

"Because I love you." He stood, took my hands, and gently pulled me into his arms. "It's my job to worry about you."

"I'm fine. I'm surrounded by people here and—as long as my parents are in town—at home too."

"How much longer are they going to be here?" he asked, lowering his head for a kiss. "Not that I'm rushing them off, but I miss cuddling on the sofa with you."

"You were too busy to do that even when they weren't here," I reminded him.

"But I knew that when I got a free evening, I could spend it with you."

"You still can." I wound my arms around his neck. "I miss you too."

As he was kissing me, Max popped in to say, "Aw, how sweet!"

I started and moved away from Jason.

"What is it?" he asked.

There was a tap on the door before Imelda came in. "Hello, hello!"

"Wow," Jason whispered. "You have incredible hearing. See you later." Giving a nod to Imelda, he went out the door.

"Oh, I do hope I'm not interrupting anything," she said.

"Only the balcony scene from *Romeo and Juliet*," Max said, raising the back of her hand to her forehead. "*My bounty is as boundless as the sea, my love as deep; the more I give to thee, the more I have, for both are infinite.*"

"Hush!" I felt my cheeks burn. "I mean, you didn't interrupt. Um...let me get that muslin for you."

Max laughed and wrapped her arms around herself in a hug.

I went into the workroom to get the muslin, convinced that one of these days someone was going to lock me up in a padded room for the things Max induced me to say and do.

When I brought out her pattern, any concern Imelda might've had over my so rudely telling her to hush evaporated with her excitement.

"Do you want me to step behind the screen and put this on?" she asked.

"Please," I said. "Let me know when you're ready for me." I quickly returned to the atelier for my wrist pin cushion.

"Ready!" Imelda called.

The muslin needed only a couple of minor alterations. While I was making them, I said, "Selma Greenfield was in earlier today trying on her muslin. Yours is a better fit than hers was."

"What color is her gown?"

"It's blue. It was meant to be green, but Selma preferred blue." I paused. "Mrs. Greenfield told me you and Violet Cross were close. I didn't realize that, and I'm terribly sorry for your loss."

"Thank you, dear. Violet and I were good friends."

"I don't mean to be indelicate, but I overheard some women gossiping in the shop earlier this week." I pinned the muslin where I'd need to add a dart to the gown. "They were talking about a falling out between Ms. Cross and the Greenfields."

Imelda stiffened. "Did you ask Selma about it?"

"No. I didn't want to be indelicate. Besides, it could have been merely hearsay."

"Right." She relaxed slightly.

I pinned a dart to the other side of the gown. "Do you know whether or not it was true? Did they argue?"

"No...no, I don't know anything about that. If you're done, dear, I should go. It's almost closing time for you, and I need to run another errand or two before I head home."

Once again, Imelda Stanbury was ducking out on me. What was she hiding?

When I got to Cassie's shop, I had to wait for her to finish up with a couple of customers. I browsed the goodies, looked longingly at a milk chocolate and toffee bar, and then talked myself out of buying it. I'd been eating far too much while Mom and Dad were home to indulge in that chocolate bar this evening. I knew I'd be back, though, sometime after they'd gone back to Florida. I'd get one for Grandpa Dave too. And one for Jason.

At last, the couple left.

"What are you up to?" Cassie asked.

"Nothing...much. I just need to borrow your key to Cross's Antiques."

"I don't get how you can talk with a ghost like it's nothing."

"It isn't nothing," I said. "It's weird actually. But one, we don't want to be haunted by this guy. And two, he could really be the key to our finding out who killed Violet Cross."

She opened the cash register, took out the key, and handed it to me. "If Mr. Justice interferes, you're interested in leasing the shop."

I nodded. "Did Jack ever say anything to you about the key?"

"No. He doesn't care. I think he's done with it and ready to pass it along to another tenant."

"Be right back." I went through Cassie's back door to Cross's Antiques, unlocked the door, and stepped inside. Despite the sun shining in through the large front window, the place struck me as looking gloomy today. "Thomas? Are you here?"

Clack, clack, clack, clack, ding!

I went over to read what he'd typed. *Where else would I be?*

"Well, Max—my friend, the ghost—you met her when—"

That was rhetorical. I'm guessing you're here because you have more questions.

"I am. Was Ms. Cross friends with Imelda Stanbury?"

Yes. Imelda came here often.

"Even after Ms. Cross severed her friendship with Selma and Stuart Greenfield?"

Yes.

"What about Dylan, Imelda's grandson?"

He came here as well occasionally—with his grandmother.

"Did you like him? Trust him?"

I had no interaction with either him or Imelda. I base my opinions of them solely on Violet's feelings. She liked and trusted them both.

I explained to Thomas as well as I could about the flash drive I found in the frame of the needlepoint portrait I'd bought here at the shop on Saturday. "Since you've met Dylan, I'm assuming it wasn't he who came in and asked Ms. Cross about the portrait on Saturday after I left."

No.

"And you have no idea where the portrait came from?" I asked. "No clue as to where it originated?"

Violet brought it in with her after church one Sunday. I supposed she was selling it for a friend. She often sold pieces on consignment like that. It was unremarkable, and we didn't discuss it.

"Did Violet and Imelda Stanbury attend the same church?"

Yes, but had Imelda intended to sell something, she'd have brought the piece here as she'd done on other occasions.

"I know you're getting tired of answering all these questions, but you must know I'm only trying to help determine who killed Ms. Cross."

I understand. If it helps, Dylan was always carrying around a small computer. He seemed unnaturally devoted to the device.

"There's a lot of that going around these days. That does help, though. Thank you." I retrieved a clean sheet of paper. "Let me know if you think of anything else."

Chapter Twenty-Three

Mom, Dad, and I had just cleaned up the kitchen after having dinner and were deciding what to watch on television when my phone rang.

"Maybe Jason got finished with the rehearsal dinner earlier than he'd expected," I said, crossing the room to pluck the phone from the charger.

But it wasn't Jason's number on the screen; it was one I didn't recognize. "Hello."

"Amanda?" a vaguely familiar voice asked.

"Yes."

"This is Selma Greenfield, and I'm at the hospital with Stu."

"Oh, no! What happened?" From the corner of my eye, I saw both Mom and Dad moving closer to me. I turned and saw the questions on their faces. I shrugged.

"He was hit on the head—hard. The emergency doctor is sewing him up now—seven stitches."

"Stitches? Yikes, what happened? Did he fall?" Seeing the fear in Dad's eyes, I muted my phone. "It's not Grandpa—something happened to one of my clients."

"Why is he calling you at home to tell you about it?" Mom asked.

"It's his wife, and I have no clue," I said. The only reason I could imagine she'd call would be to cancel the orders for their costumes. I hoped that wasn't the case, but I'd understand if it were.

"He was hit on the head with a vase," Mrs. Greenfield was saying. "We think the culprit was Imelda's grandson, Dylan."

I unmuted my line. "Where did the assault take place? What makes you think it was Dylan?"

"The incident occurred at Stu's accounting office. He was hit from behind, and while he's not a hundred percent sure Dylan was his attacker, there was a car like the one Dylan drives in the parking lot just prior to the assault. Anyway, Stu is confident enough that he wanted me to warn you."

"Warn me?" I frowned. "About what?"

"We're afraid he might come after you. Didn't you tell us you'd bought something from Violet Cross's shop?"

"Um...I think so." Did I tell them that? I wasn't sure, but it was possible.

"It's our understanding that Imelda had recently taken some things to Violet to be sold on consignment."

"And?" There had to be more to the story. "I'm having trouble following you, Mrs. Greenfield. If Dylan wanted something back that his grandmother had given to Ms. Cross to sell, then why wouldn't he have simply asked Violet to return it?"

"Stu and I suppose he hid something inside the item—like illegal drugs. I can imagine someone hiding drugs in a picture frame or a jewelry box. Can't you?"

"I guess it's possible." Possible, but not probable. Why would a teenaged boy hide a drug stash among his grandmother's possessions? It made no sense.

"I need to get back to Stu," Mrs. Greenfield said. "Please be careful."

"I will. Thank you for calling, and please give Mr. Greenfield my best." When I ended the call, I told Mom and Dad, "Well, that was weird."

"What was it?" Dad asked.

"You know the couple I'm making the Renaissance costumes for?"

He nodded. "I met them on Monday."

"Right. Someone hit Mr. Greenfield on the head at his accounting office."

"Why? Was it a client who was getting audited?" Dad asked.

Mom gave him a reproachful look before turning to me. "Is Mr. Greenfield going to be okay?"

"I believe so. He was getting stitches and might have a concussion." Not wanting to let them in on the real reason behind Mrs. Greenfield's call, I improvised. "But he might not be able to come in for his muslin fitting for a day or two."

"Why would he and his wife even be concerned about that?" Mom asked.

"These people are really serious about their Renaissance festival," I said.

"How about Amanda and I go to the grocery store and grab some snacks before we start that movie?" Dad asked.

His timing was odd—not that Dad wasn't known for his impulsiveness, but I could tell there was something else going on. "Sounds good to me. Mom, want anything in particular?"

"Only my pajamas," she said. "I'll take a bath and get comfy while the two of you are gone."

When we got into the car, Dad said, "Tell me what's really going on."

So, I did.

In the grocery store parking lot, he turned off the engine and looked at me. "What are you going to do?"

"What do you think I should do?"

"I don't know, Princess." He drummed his fingers on the steering wheel. "You were wise not to spill all this stuff in front of your mother. Not that I'm not also concerned about you, but she doesn't—and can't—know the whole story. We need to find out what's on that flash drive and determine whether or not it cost Violet Cross her life."

"Jason is already working on that. He's calling his friend Ryan, who is a deputy with the Winter Garden Sheriff's Department, to see if Ryan can find out from someone on the Abingdon police force what's on the drive."

"Good. Did Imelda or Dylan see you give the flash drive to the detective?"

Shaking my head, I said, "I had the drive in my pocket and asked the detective to step out onto the porch with me. I gave it to him outside. The only way someone would know I gave him anything would be if they were watching the building from across the street or something."

"It isn't likely someone spying on you would be obvious about it."

"I know, but even if someone did see me giving the flash drive to the police, wouldn't that be a good thing? Wouldn't that mean I'm off the hook?"

"Not necessarily," Dad said. "Whoever hid the drive in the frame might think you took a look at it first and know what's on it."

"Okay." I rubbed my forehead. "What if I call Imelda and put my cards—some of them anyway—on the table? I'll tell her I bought the portrait from Violet Cross and later understood that a young man went into her shop looking for it. I'll say it came to also came to my attention that the portrait belonged to her and that I wondered if the young man might've been Dylan."

He pressed his fist to his lips as he considered my idea. "You could say you thought it could have sen-

timental value to him and that you'd be happy to return it. If she jumps at the idea of buying the piece
back from you when she clearly didn't want it, then it
either does have some sort of meaning for Dylan—"

"Which I doubt," I interrupted.

"—or she has discovered that he hid the drive in
the frame. You did say she appeared to be searching
for something while she was in your shop yesterday."

"That's true. I'll call her tomorrow morning."

"Sounds good." He unsnapped his seatbelt. "We'd
better go in here, buy a cartload of snacks, and get
back home before your mother gets suspicious."

Two hours later, we were back at home living a
picture of domestic tranquility. Mom and Dad were
sitting on the sofa, I was curled up on the armchair,
Jazzy was snoring softly on her bed, and the movie
Yesterday was playing on the television. We were
watching the scene where the main character meets
his hero, and I was fighting tears even though I'd
already watched the film once.

My phone rang. I checked the screen. Zoe.

Dad paused the movie.

"It's Zoe," I said, unfolding my legs and getting out of the chair. "Keep the movie running. I'll be back as quickly as I can." I answered the call as I walked into the kitchen. "Zoe, is everything okay?"

"It's Maggie. I'm borrowing Zoe's phone because I don't have your number saved in mine." Her voice was hard. More so than usual.

I felt my heart speed up, and I nearly stumbled as I moved to sit on a bar stool at the island. "Wh-what's wrong?"

"Do you know a woman named Max?"

My thoughts raced. What had happened? What did Maggie know—or *think* she knew? What were Zoe and Dwight saying about this revelation? "Of course, I know Max. Why? Has something happened to her?"

With her was more likely. I needed to get a grasp on the situation as quickly as possible, but Maggie wasn't about to make it easy for me.

"What can you tell me about her?" Maggie asked.

I was losing my patience. "You need to tell me what's going on."

"I came into Zoe's room and found her video chatting with this woman."

"Okay." I drew the word out. At least, I understood what had happened now. Since Maggie was Dwight's daughter, she could see and hear Maggie just like Dwight and Zoe. Unlike them, however, Maggie didn't know Max was Dwight's aunt who'd been dead since before he was born.

"Okay?" Maggie huffed. "That's all you have to say about it? *Okay*?"

"I don't think it's all that strange." What had Zoe told her mom? I tried to tap into my inner teen. "Max is in Designs on You often, and she has become a friend to all of us."

"What does this Max person do? What does she look like? How old is she?" Maggie fired off the questions one after the other, giving me no opportunity to respond.

"Didn't you say they were video chatting?" I asked. "If so, you should already know what Max looks like."

"The woman Zoe was talking with looked like she'd hopped right out of the Roaring Twenties."

I forced out a laugh. "Good ol' Max. That's her animated...um...virtual background thingy. I don't know—it's too technical for me. I imagine Zoe could do a better job of explaining it."

"But she appeared to be in your shop," Maggie said.

"Did she?" I asked. "Huh. That must be part of the effect. I'll have to ask her how she did that. Anyway, you don't need to be concerned about Max. She's great. Ask your dad." I paused. "I mean, if you haven't already. I'm sure he can tell you as much about Max as I can."

Hopefully, he wouldn't.

"I should've known calling you wouldn't be any help at all. Goodbye."

My *goodbye* was a tad late—Maggie had already hung up. Oh, well. What was the worst that could happen? The sick feeling in the pit of my stomach told me I'd find out tomorrow morning.

Chapter Twenty-Four

rriving at work early on Friday morning, I hoped Max was around and that we'd get to talk before anyone else arrived. The parking lot was empty. Fingers crossed that Max was around. She might've spent half the night talking with Zoe after Maggie went to sleep or something.

As I got Jazzy's carrier out of the backseat of the car, I saw Max standing at my window. She raised her hand in greeting. I smiled, feeling my shoulders slump with relief. I still didn't know how much trouble Zoe was in, how we could repair this situation, or just how big a deal it was, but I knew Max was here and that we could sort through it together.

I hurried to the door. Since it was a Friday, I'd dressed casually—for the fifties. Denim pedal-pushers, a turquoise and white striped sleeveless button-down shirt tied at the waist, a sash belt made of the same material as the shirt, and white canvas sneakers.

Max popped outside. "You look like you're ready to hop on a bicycle with a basketful of flowers on the front—daisies, I think—and pedal to the village."

"Thanks." I unlocked the door. "If only I felt as carefree as you think I look."

"Yes, I know, darling. It wasn't ideal that Maggie caught Zoe and me having a chat last night. Zoe told me later that Maggie had called you."

"She did." I locked the door back behind me since I was the only one there and the shop wasn't officially open yet. I picked up the carrier and strode to Designs on You. "I'm glad you've spoken with her—is she all right?"

"Her mom was pretty steamed when she caught us. She asked Zoe who she was talking with, and Zoe said 'Max...she's my friend' like it wasn't anything out of the ordinary—because it isn't for us."

After letting Jazzy out of her carrier, I went about getting her water and kibble. "Were you talking about anything unusual? I'm trying to figure out why Maggie freaked out."

"We were just chatting." Max shrugged.

With Jazzy fed and watered, I walked into the reception area to unlock that door and to sit on one of the navy chairs. Max and Jazzy followed.

Curling my legs up under me, I said, "Maggie said it looked as if you were in my shop—"

"Of course, I was—"

"—and that you looked as if you'd stepped right out of the Roaring Twenties."

"The Roaring Twenties?" Max laughed. "I like that."

"I told her that was your animated video chat background and that I'd have to ask you how you did it," I said.

"Good comeback. I didn't even know animated video chat backgrounds were a thing."

"They are, but I don't know if Maggie bought it or not either. If Zoe told you Maggie called me, then you've spoken with Zoe since I have. How is she? Is her mom ever going to allow her to come back here?"

"We didn't have long to beat our gums," Max said. "She was afraid of getting caught. She simply called to say she's all right and that she's handling it."

"I don't like the sound of that."

Hearing the concern in my voice, Jazzy left Max's side and hopped onto my lap. She butted her head against my chin, and I rubbed my face against hers. I wished Zoe and Max had been more careful, but I didn't want to point fingers. The situation was bound to present itself at some time or another, especially with a woman who could see and hear Max just like her daughter and father could. If Maggie hadn't caught Zoe talking with Max, she could've interrupted a conversation between Max and Dwight or stopped in here and saw Max.

But why shouldn't Zoe and Dwight talk with Max? She was their relative, and they loved each other.

"When you were chatting with Zoe before Maggie interrupted, did she say anything about Dylan?" I asked.

"She said he was cute. I agreed with that, but I told her to withhold her judgment until she knows the fella better."

"Amen to that." I told her about my call from Selma Greenfield.

Max began to pace and Jazzy watched her curiously.

"Zoe told me she'd try to reach out to us when her mother went to work this morning," she said. "The only trouble with that idea is that by the time Maggie goes to work, things will start getting busy here."

"True, but Zoe is a priority. We need to find out what to do to make everything all right with Maggie."

"What *can* we do?" she asked.

"You can stop making Jazzy and me feel like we're watching the flapper-sized ball in a tennis match for starters."

"Sorry." She stopped pacing and perched on the edge of the desk. "But I can't change my appearance. Even if we do that thing where you allow me to see how I'd look wearing the clothes on the mannequin, it's still obvious I'm not a modern-day woman. I look like a woman from—well, Maggie said it herself—the Roaring Twenties."

"I know. We might simply have to tell her the truth."

"But if we do, she's likely to forbid Zoe to come here anymore."

I kissed Jazzy's head and sat her onto the floor. "That would be Maggie's choice. We'll put up a good defense, if it comes to that, but ultimately, whether Zoe is allowed to be here at Shops on Main is between her and Maggie." I stood. "Dwight will still come to visit though. I can't see Maggie being able to ground him."

"I know. But I'd miss our little Zoe."

"So would I." I went through the atelier and into the kitchen to put a pot of coffee on to brew. "I've got a feeling I'm going to need this later."

"You're summoning your nerve to call Imelda Stanbury?"

I tilted my head slightly. "Not so much summoning my nerve as trying to figure out how I'll word what I have to say."

"Do you think Mr. Greenfield really believes it was Dylan who thumped him on the melon, or is the boy simply an easy target?"

"I don't know. The Greenfields seem to be awfully defensive about Violet Cross and Imelda Stanbury. But on the other hand, Imelda and Dylan—especially Imelda—seemed to be looking for something when they were in here the other day." I filled the coffee maker with water, put the filter and ground coffee in place, and turned on the machine. "Let's go back into the reception area and see what Imelda has to say."

"I'd be having a good time with this Imelda intrigue if we knew all was well with Zoe," she said.

"I know. Hopefully, she'll call us soon." I took out my phone and called Imelda Stanbury. "Good morning, Imelda. It's Amanda Tucker from Designs on You. I hope I didn't wake you."

"Oh, no, dear, I've been up for hours."

Max shook her head. "Sounds like a sleepyhead to me."

"I'm sorry to disturb you, but Selma Greenfield called me last night and told me someone hit Stuart on the head at the accounting office," I said.

"Is Stu all right?" she asked.

"He had to have stitches—that's about all I know—but what concerned me is that Mrs. Greenfield seemed to think it had something to do with an item I bought at Cross's Antiques on Saturday."

The silence between us was palpable.

When Imelda didn't speak, I finally filled the gap. "Mrs. Greenfield said that you'd taken some items to the shop for Violet to sell on consignment. She said that later a young man went to Cross's Antiques, inquired about the item, and was told that I'd bought it."

"How would Selma know that?" Imelda's voice was hoarse when she spoke.

"I don't know," I said. "But I wanted to tell you that I bought a needlepoint portrait that day and that if it does indeed have some value to you or to

Dylan—if maybe you hadn't intended for it to be sold—I'll gladly let you have it back."

"You don't honestly believe Dylan hit Stu Greenfield over the head because of a needlepoint portrait, do you?" Imelda asked. "I don't know where Selma is getting her ideas or why she's insisting on maligning me, my friends, and my family, but I intend to see to it that her harassment ends here and now."

"I don't blame you in the least. But, for my own peace of mind, did the portrait belong to you? And does Dylan want it back for some reason?"

Again, Imelda was quiet for a long moment. "The portrait was mine. It was done by my late sister. I've always found it rather depressing, so I gave it to Violet to sell on consignment. I'll check with Dylan to see if it was he who inquired after it in the antique shop...though I don't know why he would."

"Thank you."

"I'll let you know," she said. "Goodbye."

"Good—" *Click.* I glanced at Max. "She hung up."

"So I gathered. Now what?"

"Now we wait."

It was nearly noon when Dwight and Zoe came to visit.

"We got in trouble," Dwight said, with an impish grin.

"Yes, we did, and it wasn't very funny." Zoe came into the workroom, dropped her backpack onto the table, and slumped onto a chair. "Mom was mad."

"Why?" Max asked. "What did we do that was so awful? Amanda said she tried to explain away my appearance and my being here at the shop as a...a trick or something."

"Yeah, that was good thinking," Zoe told me. "And Mom kinda bought it, but then she asked why we hadn't told her anything about Max before now."

"I said she wasn't terribly keen on you, Amanda, and that we thought she might not approve of your friends either." Dwight nodded when he'd finished the sentence as if he were particularly proud of himself.

"I imagine that helped." I was being sarcastic.

"No, actually, it made things worse," Dwight said.

"Give us the straight dope," Max said. "Is she going to allow you to keep your part-time job here?"

Zoe sank a little lower into her chair. "Who knows?"

"She wants to meet you," Dwight said to Max.

"And why shouldn't she?" Max asked. "We're family."

With a groan, Zoe said, "She'll never accept you."

"You don't know that." Max grinned. "Who wouldn't want to be friends with me?"

I had a feeling that was sinking lower than Zoe into her chair that we were soon to find out.

Chapter Twenty-Five

Not long after Dwight and Zoe arrived at Designs on You, Mom and Dad came in.

"Hello, all," Dad greeted. "You don't look like much of a lively group on this sunny Friday."

"Been a long week, David," Dwight said. "How are you? Are you missing Florida yet?"

"No, I'm—" Dad began.

"I am," Mom said, speaking overtop of Dad. "Mandy, did you hear anything from Jason this morning? Are we going to lunch with him?"

"Let me text him and see if he's available." I took out my phone.

"Would you and Zoe like to join us?" Dad asked.

"Thank you for the invitation, but someone should be here to watch the store." Dwight winked. "And it's gonna be Zoe because I'm planning to see what's new at the shops today."

"Don't tempt me, or I might stay here with you." Dad grinned. "At least, tell me what I can bring you back."

"I wouldn't turn down a burger or a sandwich." Dwight jerked his head toward Zoe. "I doubt she would either."

"Consider it done."

I'd stepped into the hallway to text Jason, and Max came to stand by my side.

"Zoe doesn't seem in the mood for company, so I'm going to pop out and rest for a while." She sighed. "I might have a big afternoon ahead of me."

"Don't worry overmuch about Zoe," I whispered. "She'll be fine."

"Did you hear back from him?" Mom asked, at my side. She'd have plowed Max over had Max been cor-poreal. She rubbed her arms. "It's cold here in the hall. Is there a problem with the thermostat?"

"It's fine, Mom. And, no, I haven't heard back yet. I just—"

My phone buzzed. It was the reply from Jason.

I read it and looked at Mom. "He'll meet us at the sandwich shop in ten minutes."

"We'd better grab your Dad and go then."

"Go ahead," I said. "I'll check and see if anyone else wants anything."

Jason was waiting for us at the sandwich shop. He stood, hugged me, greeted Mom, and shook Dad's hand before we walked to the counter to order.

"I need to snap a couple photos of you in that outfit," Jason said, as we waited our turn.

I laughed. "Max said I looked as if I should be bicycling through a village with a basketful of daisies."

Dad's eyes widened.

"Who's Max?" Mom asked.

"She's a woman who comes into the shop sometimes," I said.

"Yeah, I met her." Dad was eager to help. "She's a real character."

"I'll snap some pics of the three of you after lunch, if you'd like," Jason said.

"I'd like that very much," I said.

"I don't know." Mom patted her head. "My hair is a mess today."

"Mom, it's fine."

Although it felt like three days' later but was only something like seven minutes, we got our food and sat back down.

"Oh, hey," Jason said, as he placed a straw into his cup. "I heard back from Ryan. That computer flash drive you found contained two copies of some sort of ledger—one apparently legitimate and the other a fake. Ryan said the Abingdon police are investigating it further but that it's highly suspicious."

"What computer flash drive?" Mom asked. "What's going on?"

"It's...it's not that big a deal—" I began.

"Not that big a deal? Then what are the police doing with it?" She looked from me to Dad.

"Amanda found the drive after the break-in and turned it over to the police," Dad said.

"Right." I smiled slightly. Dad had come through in a pinch—again.

"How come you knew about this, but I didn't?" Mom folded her arms across her chest.

So much for Dad getting us out of this mess.

"We talked about it last night on our way to the store," I said. "Remember, you didn't want to go—you stayed at home and took a bath."

"You two seem to enjoy shutting me out."

"We didn't mean to exclude you." I placed my hand on her arm, but she jerked it away. "We didn't want to worry you unnecessarily."

Jason gave me a look of sympathy as he ducked his head. "It sure is gorgeous weather we're having today. Probably milder than what you're used to in Florida." He took a bite of his sandwich.

"Yeah, I enjoy the more temperate climate," Dad said. "Terri prefers the heat of Florida. I'd love to stay here another month, but unfortunately, I have to be back at work on Wednesday."

The rest of that lunch was about as awkward as the first part—all of us, except Mom, eating and trying to make noncommittal small talk. She did neither, preferring to sulk.

When I delivered Connie her ham and Swiss on rye after we returned to Shops on Main, she could immediately tell something was wrong.

Her shop empty at the moment, she asked, "Wanna talk about it?"

Smiling slightly, I said, "Are you sure you want to hear about it?"

"I'm all ears." She sat on the stool behind her counter, poured some tea into a cup from her thermos, and unwrapped her sandwich.

I told her about lunch, even including the part about the computer flash drive I'd given to the police.

"We didn't even pose for the photographs Jason had offered to take for us," I concluded. "Everyone was in too much of a mood."

"He can take them later," she said. "And don't be so hard on your mom. It's difficult for us sometimes—dads seem to always be the fun parents. It's like that at my house anyway. I'm the nag who tells the kids to clean their rooms and get their homework done and eat their vegetables. Will is the one who suggests we get pizza, brings home new movies and games, and plans spur-of-the-moment trips."

"I understand." I was actually thinking that maybe Connie should take the initiative to be the more carefree parent once in a while. "Mom is more of a worrier than Dad. We didn't want her to be concerned with something that might ruin her time here—the break-in was scary enough on its own."

Connie nodded. "Maybe the two of you could do something special together while your dad and grandpa keep each other company tomorrow or Sunday afternoon."

"Maybe." I jerked my head in the direction of my shop. "I'd better get back—Zoe will think I've gotten lost."

Zoe didn't think I'd gotten lost. She more accurately concluded that I'd been hiding until after Mom and Dad left.

"I have to say your mom and mine rank pretty close in the bad mom department," she said.

"I wouldn't say either of them are bad." I sat beside her. "They care about us, are overprotective, and don't always know how to show their affection."

"Uh, and they're neurotic; they get on our nerves; and they don't give us any credit for having common sense."

"You've got me there," I said.

Jazzy rubbed against my ankles, and I stroked her head. I silently watched Zoe work for a moment—her long, thin fingers twisting three strands of silver metal into a braid.

"Say it," she said at last.

Not even pretending I didn't understand, I said, "All right. I'm leaving the decision up to you, but I feel it's time to introduce your mom to Max. If Maggie can't handle it, that's all right."

"It's not all right! You and Max are the best friends I have. I can't lose you!"

"You won't. I promise you that." I placed a hand lightly on her forearm. "We'll always be here for you. I just think it will be a lot easier for all of us in the long run if your mother knows about Max."

Zoe sighed and then tightened her lips. "But Max is a—" She looked around for a moment to make sure no one was coming into the shop. "—a ghost."

"True, but your mother can see and hear her. That's a much better situation than the one I'm in. If I told my mom about Max, she'd think Max was merely something else Dad and I could share without her. She'd believe we made Max up to taunt her. At least, Maggie knows Max is real."

"But she won't."

Raising my hands in mock surrender, I said, "We'll handle this situation however you'd like. Introducing Maggie to Max is only one alternative."

"Well, it's a bad idea."

Dwight returned to the shop with bags of presents for all of us that he'd bought from the other vendors in the building. "Where are Terri and David?"

"They've gone home already," I said.

"Did lunch not agree with them?" He frowned.

"Something like that."

He clapped me on the shoulder. "We'll all be all right. You know what they say—life is always rocky when you're a gem."

Imelda and Dylan came in later that afternoon. I was alone, except for a client who'd come in looking for a strapless gown like the one worn by Rita Hayworth in *The Lady from Shanghai*.

"I'll be right with you," I told Imelda and Dylan.

"You don't have anything like that gown off-the-rack?" the woman asked. "I was hoping to wear it this weekend."

"No, that would be a custom design," I said. "Maybe you'll find something else to your liking from the ready-to-wear line."

"I don't think so." With a sniff, she left the shop.

"She seemed rude," Imelda said.

"I get people like that sometimes. They want something to practically appear for them magically," I said.

"And for little cost, I'm guessing," she added.

"Your guess is correct." I smiled. "It's nice to see both of you again."

"Nice to see you," Dylan said. "Where's Zoe today?"

"She's already left for the day, but I'll tell her you asked about her," I said.

"Thanks. Um...about that needlepoint portrait." He shoved his hands into his pockets and looked down at his shoes. "I'm embarrassed to admit that I had my friend Steve go into the shop and ask about it. When I was little, I thought the kid in the portrait was me—that my great-aunt Sosie had made it for me."

"I had no clue the portrait had been special to Dylan," Imelda said. "Could we please have it back?" She took out her wallet. "I'm happy to reimburse you."

"Thank you. I'm glad the portrait is going back to where it belongs," I said.

"So are we." Dylan and his grandmother exchanged glances.

I wasn't sure if it was the portrait or the flash drive they might still believe was secreted in the side of the frame that was important to them. But, at this point, it didn't matter all that much. I'd done everything I could do to help Thomas Wortley discover who'd murdered Violet Cross and why. As far as I was concerned, the police could carry on the investigation now without my assistance—or, more accurately, my inept interference. I planned to spend the weekend with my parents tomorrow and, hopefully, be able to see my boyfriend too.

Figuratively washing my hands of the affair, I went to the atelier and took a seat at my favorite sewing machine.

Chapter Twenty-Six

A round closing time, I was surprised to get a call from Imelda.

"Hi, Amanda," she said. "Would you mind staying open a few minutes longer in order to measure Dylan for a Renaissance festival costume? I feel I need to get him in there before he changes his mind."

"Um...sure." I didn't want to stay open late on a Friday afternoon, but I didn't want to alienate a client. Plus, if either of them felt the need to share something about that portrait, I wanted to know. I mean, sure, I'd already written off the case; but if there was anything Imelda or Dylan would like to clear up for me...

I felt confident Dylan had been the one who'd hidden the flash drive in the frame. But, of course, I could be wrong. Maybe he *was* sentimental about the portrait because his great-aunt had made it for him. Or maybe my first impression had been correct. Either way, I could hopefully get some answers.

I texted Dad that I was running later that I'd expected today.

Max showed up just as I pressed *Send*.

"I've got a bad feeling," she said.

I did too, but I didn't want to be overly dramatic. "It'll be all right."

"What was on that device you found hidden in the picture frame?"

"Two ledgers." I watched from the window as the Petermans crossed the parking lot and got into their vehicle. Other than Ford and me, they were the last ones here. "Apparently, one was the true ledger and the other was a dummy."

"What were these ledgers for?" she asked. "The Renaissance organization?"

"I don't know—Jason didn't give me that information, and I'm guessing Ryan didn't give it to him." I shrugged slightly. "The police might not even know for sure at this point."

"The entire embezzlement scheme is a hard mouthful to swallow, don't you think?" Max settled above the wingback chair beside me. "Let's say we have this criminal mastermind Violet Cross stealing money and cooking the books over at the Renaissance organization. If she was so savvy, how did the Greenfields catch her?"

"I've never believed the story of Violet embezzling money." There went Ford. Now Max and I were alone in the building. Wonder if anyone had locked the door? Probably not. "I believe someone was trying to make Violet their scapegoat."

"Who'd do that?" Max asked. "Dylan? Do you think he'd steal the money, funnel it wherever he needed it to go, and then use these dummy ledgers to cover his tracks?"

Shaking my head, I said, "It doesn't make sense. If he's clever enough to steal money that way, then he'd know how to encrypt the files, use a digital wallet, or somehow make his transactions more difficult to trace than a person who'd write everything down in two separate ledgers."

"Who then?" Max lay back across the chair, stared up at the ceiling, and scissored her legs. "Imelda?"

I, too, stared up at the ceiling and considered the evidence. "The Greenfields have their own business—the accounting firm—plus, they're heads of the Southern Appalachian Renaissance Society. Huh..."

Max sat up. "Huh, what?"

"Well, if they wanted to, the Renaissance organization would provide the perfect cover for them to move funds back and forth between the two accounts. Think about it. Too much revenue for the business and you need to shelter it to reduce your tax burden? Move it over to the nonprofit."

"Shush!" Max nodded toward the window. "They're here."

"Who's here?" I asked. By the time I'd glanced at the window, the people who'd gotten out of the SUV were gone. "Dylan and Imelda?"

"Yes, dear, we're here!" Imelda called.

"Something's off." Max put herself between me and the door.

Even though there was nothing she could do to protect me, I appreciated the gesture.

"Come on in." I opened the reception room door to find Dylan, Imelda, and the Greenfields. "This is a surprise."

"More like a shock," Max said. "I thought he accused the kid of smashing in his melon."

Stuart Greenfield did have a gauze patch on the side of his head.

"How are you feeling, Mr. Greenfield?" I asked.

"I've been better." He gave me a wan smile. "Thank you for your concern."

I looked from him to Dylan and back. "I never expected to see all four of you together after Mrs. Greenfield's call last night, but I trust you've worked out your differences."

"Play it cool, darling," Max said softly. "I'm very afraid for you."

"I did believe Dylan had something that belonged to Selma and me," Mr. Greenfield said. "It's something we're desperate to have returned."

"So desperate I had to smash a vase over Stu's head to force Dylan's hand." Mrs. Greenfield bit her lip. "Unfortunately, it didn't work because Dylan doesn't have it." She narrowed her eyes at me, and her voice hardened. "Where is it?"

"Where's what?" I asked.

Mrs. Greenfield advanced on me. Max stood between us, and I could see the goosebumps rise on Mrs. Greenfield's flesh from the burst of cold. I wish she could see Max...or hear her. That might buy me enough time to get out of here. But what about

Imelda and Dylan? They were sharing the boat with me. I couldn't simply abandon ship.

I caught Max's eye. "Nine...one...one."

She nodded and disappeared.

"What are you mumbling?" Mrs. Greenfield asked.

"The police are on their way," I said. "I don't know what you believe I've taken from you, but I have nothing of interest to you here. Your threats won't produce anything, and the police are on their way."

"Dylan told us he put a flash drive in the picture frame of the portrait you bought at Violet Cross's antique shop," Mr. Greenfield said. "It's not there now. What did you do with it?"

"I turned it over to the police after the break-in," I said.

Selma Greenfield elbowed her husband in the sternum. "You idiot! I told you hiring those imbeciles to break in here was a stupid idea. It only served to put her on alert. We could've gotten that portrait the way we did today, and no one would've ever been the wiser."

I backed away from Mrs. Greenfield until my legs hit the back of my desk. "What's your plan now? Are you going to hit us all on the back of the head like you did Violet Cross?"

"Violet was an accident," Mr. Greenfield said. "We aren't killers."

"Shut up, Stu! We're not going down for this!" Mrs. Greenfield's glare turned from her husband back to me. "What did you really do with that flash drive?"

"I gave it to the detective." I nodded toward Imelda. "She knows. She and Dylan were here when the detective arrived. I took him out onto the porch to give him the drive."

"You didn't tell me what you were doing," Imelda said. "I wish Dylan and I had never gotten caught up in this mess."

"But you did! All of you did because you didn't have the good sense to mind your own business!"

Amid Mrs. Greenfield's ranting, my mother flung open the door. "Enough is enough!"

She'd spoken so forcefully that both Mr. and Mrs. Greenfield raised their hands defensively.

"I don't know what's going on around here, but we came all the way from Florida to spend some time with our daughter," Mom continued. "I realize she has a business to run, but she also needs to make time to spend with her family. Whatever it is you're doing can wait until tomorrow."

Mrs. Greenfield gaped at Mom for a few still seconds. Then she said, "No, actually, it can't." She took a small gun from her purse and pointed it at Mom.

"Hey! That's my mother!" I shouted.

"Shut up!" Mrs. Greenfield yelled. "I need to think!" She jerked her head toward my desk. "Get over there—all of you."

Mom, Dylan, and Imelda joined me in front of the desk. Mom squeezed my hand.

"About a minute out," Max said from somewhere behind me.

I nodded slightly, realizing I needed to keep Mrs. Greenfield talking—and not shooting us—for a full minute. "How did everything fall apart?"

"Him." Mrs. Greenfield spat the word in Dylan's direction. "He had to go nosing into everything while Violet was sick. 'Dylan is an enterprising boy. He'll be happy to fill in,' Imelda said. Oh, he was happy to do it all right."

"Hey, it's not my fault you're crooks," Dylan said.

Imelda grabbed his arm. "Hush!" To the Greenfields, she said, "He didn't mean that."

"Mandy, I'm sorry," Mom said. "I've not always been the most understanding mother, but I love you. I want you to know that."

"Mom, I do—"

Before I could finish my thought, Mom dived across the floor and tackled Selma Greenfield. The gun clattered under the desk, and Dylan scrambled to pick it up.

"Nobody move!"

The police had arrived and were apparently having a hard time discerning who were the good guys and who were the bad guys. We all held up our hands and did as we were told. Except for Max. She was laughing too hard.

Chapter Twenty-Seven

On Saturday morning, Mom and Dad stayed home. Although I needed to work for a few hours, Mom and I had plans for later, and Dad and Grandpa were going fishing. I was happy the Violet Cross ordeal was behind me...for the most part. I still needed to go talk with Thomas Wortley after work.

Zoe and Maggie came in first thing.

Closing the door behind her, Zoe asked, "Is Max here?"

"I haven't seen her this morning." It was true. I imagined Max was still resting up after yesterday's excitement.

"I want my mom to meet her," Zoe said.

Appearing in the atelier and walking toward them, Max said, "And I want to meet her." She smiled. "Hello, Maggie."

"Wh-where did you come from?" Maggie asked.

"I was around."

"Let's all go into the atelier," I said. That way, if any customers came in, the three of them could remain in the workroom while I entertained the customers in the reception area. "Maggie would you like some coffee?"

"No, thank you." Maggie gave Max an appraising glance. "That's what you were wearing when you were chatting with Zoe the other day."

"That's right."

"Why?" Maggie asked.

"It's what she wears," Zoe said.

I gave Zoe a subtle headshake to encourage her to let her mom and Max navigate these waters together.

Maggie inclined her head. "You aren't...normal, are you?"

Max laughed. "Hardly. I do adore your daughter and your father though, and I'd like to get to know you as well. We're related, you know."

"How?"

After looking at me and Zoe, Max shrugged. "I'm your father's aunt. Dorothy—Dot—was my sister."

Someone came into the reception area, and I went to see who it was. I pulled the door closed behind me.

Our merry band of animal lovers tramped from Alvarado Station along the Virginia Creeper Trail to the Historic Abingdon Donkey Lodge. Mom and I were in the lead, followed by Maggie, Zoe, Connie, and her daughter Marielle.

We'd decided on the spur of the moment Friday evening—after Mom's and my confrontation with the Greenfields and subsequent police investigation—to do something fun just for us gals. I'd invited Connie, who was easily persuaded to be the spontaneous parent for a change. And this morning I'd encouraged Maggie and Zoe to go. I planned to keep hammering away at Maggie's tough exterior until she let me in and decided she liked me—at least, a little. For now, it was enough that she'd agreed to let Zoe continue working at Designs on You. We'd take everything else a baby step at a time.

Christal, the host of the miniature donkey experience, welcomed us and set out a few ground rules—namely, don't walk up behind the donkeys and don't make any loud or sudden noises. Some of the rescued animals had PTSD.

I quickly fell in love with Robbie, a standard-sized donkey who enjoyed resting his head on my shoulder. Mom and Zoe preferred the minatures—Buck and Frosty, in particular—while Maggie showed a particular fondness for Ruthanne, the mammoth donkey. Connie and Marielle adored them all.

"Mom, I want one!" Marielle cried.

"Let's keep visiting these instead," Connie said. "That way, you can be friends with all of them."

Robbie raised his head from my shoulder and looked me in the eye.

"You're such a sweetheart," I whispered. "There's a story I could tell you about a typewriting ghost who crossed over to the other side this morning after I told him the people responsible for the death of the woman he loves have been brought to justice, but you'd never believe me."

At that, Robbie brayed right in my ear.

Author's Notes

You're the elephant's eyebrows!

Thank you so much for taking the time to read this book! I hope you've enjoyed it, and I'm grateful for your support and encouragement.

Here are links to all (or, at least, some) of the wonderful things mentioned in *Buttons and Blows*:

Downhearted Blues - https://youtu.be/go6TiLIeVZA

Abingdon Gifting Co. - https://abingdongiftingco.com/

Macbeth Tartan -
https://www.scotlandshop.com/us/tartan-finder/macbeth

Abingdon Railroad -
https://vacreepertrail.com/history/vacreeperhistory.htm

Hugh Allan -
https://www.imdb.com/name/nm0019935/

Anthony's Desserts -
https://www.anthonysdesserts.com/

Suspicious Minds - https://youtu.be/Y_RCvsiavuM

E. C. Brewster Clocks -
https://www.pbs.org/wgbh/roadshow/season/15/des-moines-ia/appraisals/ec-brewster-beehive-clock-ca-1838--201005A22/

Historic Abingdon Donkey Lodge -
https://donkeylodge.com/

ABOUT THE AUTHOR

Gayle Leeson is a pseudonym for Gayle Trent. I also write as Amanda Lee. As Gayle Trent, I write the Daphne Martin Cake Mystery series and the Myrtle Crumb Mystery series. As Amanda Lee, I write the Embroidery Mystery series. To eliminate confusion going forward, I'm writing under the name Gayle Leeson only. My family and I live in Virginia near Abingdon, Virginia, and I'm having a blast with this series.

If you enjoyed this book, Gayle would appreciate your leaving a review. If you don't know what to say, there is a handy book review guide at her site (https://www.gayleleeson.com/book-review-form). Gayle invites you to sign up for her newsletter and receive excerpts of some of her books: https://forms.aweber.com/form/14/1780369214.htm

Social Media Links:
Twitter:

https://twitter.com/GayleTrent

Facebook:

https://www.facebook.com/GayleLeeson/

BookBub:

https://www.bookbub.com/profile/gayle-leeson

Goodreads:

https://www.goodreads.com/author/show/426208.Gayle_Trent

Have you read the first book in the Ghostly Fashionista series?

Excerpt from *Designs on Murder*

Chapter One

A flash of brilliant light burst from the lower righthand window of Shops on Main, drawing my attention to the FOR LEASE sign. I'd always loved the building and couldn't resist going inside to see the space available.

I opened the front door to the charming old mansion, which had started life as a private home in the late 1800s and had had many incarnations since then. I turned right to open another door to go into the vacant office.

"Why so glum, chum?" asked a tall, attractive woman with a dark brown bob and an impish grin.

She stood near the window wearing a rather fancy mauve gown for the middle of the day. She was also wearing a headband with a peacock feather, making her look like a flapper from the 1920s. I wondered if she might be going to some sort of party after work. Either that, or this woman was quite the eccentric.

"I just came from a job interview," I said.

"Ah. Don't think it went well, huh?"

"Actually, I think it did. But I'm not sure I want to be doing that kind of work for...well...forever."

"Nothing's forever, darling. But you've come to the right place. My name's Max, by the way. Maxine, actually, but I hate that stuffy old name. Maxine Englebright. Isn't that a mouthful? You can see why I prefer Max."

I chuckled. "It's nice to meet you, Max. I'm Amanda Tucker."

"So, Amanda Tucker," Max said, moving over to the middle of the room, "what's your dream job?"

"I know it'll sound stupid. I shouldn't have even wandered in here--"

"Stop that please. Negativity gets us nowhere."

Max sounded like a school teacher then, and I tried to assess her age. Although she somehow seemed older, she didn't look much more than my twenty-four years. I'd put her at about thirty...if that. Since she was looking at me expectantly, I tried to give a better answer to her question.

"I want to fill a niche...to make some sort of difference," I said. "I want to do something fun, exciting...something I'd look forward to doing every day."

"And you're considering starting your own business?"

"That was my initial thought upon seeing that this space is for lease. I love this building...always have."

"What sort of business are you thinking you'd like to put here?" Max asked.

"I enjoy fashion design, but my parents discouraged me because—they said—it was as hard to break into as professional sports. I told them there are a lot of people in professional sports, but they said, 'Only the best, Mandy.'"

Max gave an indignant little bark. "Oh, that's hooey! But I can identify. My folks never thought I'd amount to much. Come to think of it, I guess I didn't." She threw back her head and laughed.

"Oh, well, I wish I could see some of your designs."

"You can. I have a couple of my latest right here on my phone." I took my cell phone from my purse and pulled up the two designs I'd photographed the day before. The first dress had a small pink and green floral print on a navy background, shawl collar, three-quarter length sleeves, and A-line skirt. "I love vintage styles."

"This is gorgeous! I'd love to have a dress like this."

"Really?"

"Yeah. What else ya got?" Max asked.

My other design was an emerald 1930s-style bias cut evening gown with a plunging halter neckline and a back panel with pearl buttons that began at the middle of the back on each side and went to the waist.

Max caught her breath. "That's the berries, kid!"

"Thanks." I could feel the color rising in my cheeks. Max might throw out some odd phrases, but I could tell she liked the dress. "Mom and Dad are probably right, though. Despite the fact that I use modern fabrics—some with quirky, unusual patterns—how could I be sure I'd have the clientele to actually support a business?"

"Are you kidding me? People would love to have their very own fashion designer here in little ol' Abingdon."

"You really think so? Is it the kind of place you'd visit?" I asked.

"Visit?" Max laughed. "Darling, I'd practically live in it."

"All right. I'll think about it."

"Think quickly please. There was someone in here earlier today looking at the space. He wants to sell cigars and tobacco products. Pew. The smell would drive me screwy. I'd much rather have you here."

Hmm...the lady had her sales pitch down. I had to give her that. "How much is the rent?"

"Oh, I have no idea. You'll find Mrs. Meacham at the top of the stairs, last door on your left. It's marked OFFICE."

"Okay. I'll go up and talk with her."

"Good luck, buttercup!"

I was smiling and shaking my head as I mounted the stairs. Max was a character. I thought she'd be a fun person to have around.

Since the office wasn't a retail space like the other rooms in the building, I knocked and waited for a response before entering.

Mrs. Meacham was a plump, prim woman with short, curly white hair and sharp blue eyes. She looked at me over the top of her reading glasses. "How may I help you?"

"I'm interested in the space for rent downstairs," I said.

"You are? Oh, my! I thought you were here selling cookies or something. You look so young." Mrs. Meacham laughed at her own joke, so I faked a chortle to be polite. "What type of shop are you considering?"

"A fashion boutique."

"Fashion?"

"Yes, I design and create retro-style fashions."

"Hmm. I never picked up sewing myself. I've never been big on crafts." She stood and opened a file cabinet to the left of her desk, and I could see she was wearing a navy suit. "Canning and baking were more my strengths. I suppose you could say I prefer the kitchen to the hearth." She laughed again, and I chuckled along with her.

She turned and handed me an application. "Just read this over and call me back if you have any questions. If you're interested in the space, please let me know as soon as possible. There's a gentleman interested in opening a cigar store there." She tapped a pen on her desk blotter. "But even if he gets here before you do, we'll have another opening by the first of the month. The web designer across the hall is leaving. Would you like to take a look at his place before you decide?"

"No, I'd really prefer the shop on the ground floor," I said.

"All right. Well, I hope to hear from you soon."

I left then. I stopped back by the space for lease to say goodbye to Max, but she was gone.

I went home—my parents' home actually, but they moved to Florida for Dad's job more than two years ago, so it was basically mine...until they wanted it back. I made popcorn for lunch, read over Mrs. Meacham's contract, and started crunching the numbers.

I'd graduated in May with a bachelor's degree in business administration with a concentration in marketing and entrepreneurship but just couldn't find a position that sparked any sort of passion in me. This morning I'd had yet another interview where I'd been overqualified for the position but felt I had a good chance of getting an offer...a low offer...for work I couldn't see myself investing decades doing.

Jasmine, my cat, wandered into the room. She'd eaten some kibble from her bowl in the kitchen and was now interested in what I was having. She hopped onto the coffee table, peeped into the popcorn bowl, and turned away dismissively to clean her paws. She was a beautiful gray and white striped tabby. Her feet were white, and she looked as if she were wearing socks of varying lengths—crew socks on the back, anklets on the front.

"What do you think, Jazzy?" I asked. "Should I open a fashion boutique?"

She looked over her shoulder at me for a second before resuming her paw-licking. I didn't know if that was a yes or a no.

Even though I'd gone to school for four years to learn all about how to open, manage, and provide inventory for a small business, I researched for the remainder of the afternoon. I checked out the stats on independent designers in the United States and fashion boutiques in Virginia. There weren't many in the Southwest Virginia region, so I knew I'd have something unique to offer my clientele.

Finally, Jazzy let me know that she'd been napping long enough and that we needed to do something. Mainly, I needed to feed her again, and she wanted to eat. But I had other ideas.

"Jazzy, let's get your carrier. You and I are going to see Grandpa Dave."

Grandpa Dave was my favorite person on the planet, and Jazzy thought pretty highly of him herself. He lived only about ten minutes away from us. He was farther out in the country and had a bigger home than we did. Jazzy and I were happy in our little three-bedroom, one bath ranch. We secretly hoped Dad wouldn't lose the job that had taken him and Mom to Florida and that they'd love it too much to leave when he retired because we'd gotten used to having the extra space.

I put the carrier on the backseat of my green sedan. It was a cute car that I'd worked the summer between high school and college to get enough money to make the down payment on, but it felt kinda ironic to be driving a cat around in a car that reminded people of a hamster cage.

Sometimes, I wished my Mom and Dad's house was a bit farther from town. It was so peaceful out here in the country. Fences, pastureland, and cows bordered each side of the road. There were a few houses here and there, but most of the land was still farmland. The farmhouses were back off the road and closer to the barns.

When we pulled into Grandpa Dave's long drive-way, Jazzy meowed.

"Yes," I told her. "We're here."

Grandpa Dave lived about fifty yards off the road, and his property was fenced, but he didn't keep any animals. He'd turned the barn that had been on the land when he and Grandma Jodie bought it into a workshop where he liked to "piddle."

I pulled around to the side of the house and was happy to see that, rather than piddling in the work-shop, Grandpa was sitting on one of the white rock-ing chairs on the porch. I parked and got out, opened the door to both the car and the carrier for Jazzy, and she ran straight to hop onto his lap.

"Well, there's my girls!" Grandpa Dave laughed.

It seemed to me that Grandpa was almost always laughing. He'd lost a little of that laughter after Grandma Jodie had died. But that was five years ago, and, except for some moments of misty remem-brance, he was back to his old self.

I gave him a hug and a kiss on the cheek before settling onto the swing.

"I was sorta expecting you today," he said. "How'd the interview go?"

"It went fine, I guess, but I'm not sure Integrated Manufacturing Technologies is for me. The boss was nice, and the offices are beautiful, but...I don't know."

"What ain't she telling me, Jazzy?"

The cat looked up at him adoringly before butting her head against his chin.

"I'm...um...I'm thinking about starting my own business." I didn't venture a glance at Grandpa Dave right away. I wasn't sure I wanted to know what he was thinking. I figured he was thinking I'd come to ask for money--which I had, money and advice—but I was emphatic it was going to be a loan.

Grandpa had already insisted on paying my college tuition and wouldn't hear of my paying him back. This time, I was giving him no choice in the matter. Either he'd lend me the money, and sign the loan agreement I'd drafted, or I wouldn't take it.

I finally raised my eyes to look at his face, and he was looking pensive.

"Tell me what brought this on," he said.

I told him about wandering into Shops on Main after my interview and meeting Maxine Englebright. "She loved the designs I showed her and seemed to think I could do well if I opened a boutique there. I went upstairs and got an application from the building manager, and then I went home and did some research. I'd never seriously considered opening my own business before--at least, not at this stage of my career--but I'd like to try."

Another glance at Grandpa Dave told me he was still listening but might take more convincing.

"I realize I'm young, and I'm aware that more than half of all small businesses fail in the first four years. But I've got a degree that says I'm qualified to manage a business. Why not manage my own?"

He remained quiet.

"I know that opening a fashion boutique might seem frivolous, but there aren't a lot of designers in this region. I believe I could fill a need...or at least a niche."

Grandpa sat Jazzy onto the porch and stood. Without a word, he went into the house.

Jazzy looked up at me. *Meow?* She went over to the door to see where Grandpa Dave went. *Meow?* She stood on her hind legs and peered through the door.

"Watch out, Jasmine," he said, waiting for her to hop down and back away before he opened the door. He was carrying his checkbook. "How much do you need?"

"Well, I have some savings, and—"

"That's not what I asked."

"Okay. Now, this will be a loan, Grandpa Dave, not a gift."

"If you don't tell me how much, I'm taking this checkbook back into the house, and we won't discuss it any further."

"Ten thousand dollars," I blurted.

As he was writing the check, he asked, "Have you and Jazzy had your dinner yet?"

We were such frequent guests that he kept her favorite cat food on hand.

"We haven't. Do you have the ingredients to make a pizza?"

He scoffed. "Like I'm ever without pizza-makings." He handed me the check. "By the way, how old is this Max you met today? She sounds like quite a gal."

"She doesn't look all that much older than me. But she seems more worldly...or something. I think you'd like her," I said. "But wait, aren't you still seeing Betsy?"

He shrugged. "Betsy is all right to take to Bingo...but this Max sounds like she could be someone special."

First thing the next morning, I went to the bank to set up a business account for Designs on You. That's what I decided to name my shop. Then I went to Shops on Main and gave Mrs. Meacham my application. After she made sure everything was in order, she took my check for the first month's rent and then took me around to meet the rest of the shop owners.

She introduced me to the upstairs tenants first. There was Janice, who owned Janice's Jewelry. She was of average height but she wore stilettos, had tawny hair with blonde highlights, wore a shirt that was way too tight, and was a big fan of dermal fillers, given her expressionless face.

"Janice, I'd like you to meet Amanda," said Mrs. Meacham. "She's going to be opening a fashion boutique downstairs."

"Fashion? You and I should talk, Amanda. You dress them, and I'll accessorize them." She giggled before turning to pick up a pendant with a large, light green stone. "With your coloring, you'd look lovely in one of these Amazonite necklace and earring sets."

"I'll have to check them out later," I said. "It was nice meeting you."

Janice grabbed a stack of her business cards and pressed them into my hand. "Here. For your clients. I'll be glad to return the favor."

"Great. Thanks."

Next, Mrs. Meacham took me to meet Mark, a web site designer. Everything about Mark screamed thin. The young man didn't appear to have an ounce of fat on his body. He had thinning black hair. He wore a thin crocheted tie. He held out a thin hand for me to shake. His handshake was surprisingly firm.

"Hello. It's a pleasure to meet you, Amanda." He handed me a card from the holder on his desk. "Should you need any web design help or marketing expertise, please call on me. I can work on a flat fee or monthly fee basis, depending on your needs."

"Thank you, but—"

"Are you aware that fifty percent of fledgling businesses fail within the first year?" he asked.

I started to correct his stats, but I didn't want to alienate someone I was going to be working near. I thanked him again and told him I appreciated his offer. It dawned on me as Mrs. Meacham and I were moving on to the next tenant that she'd said the web designer was leaving at the end of the month...which was only a week away. I wondered where he was taking his business.

The other upstairs shop was a bookstore called Antiquated Editions. The owner was a burly, bearded man who'd have looked more at home in a motorcycle shop than selling rare books, but, hey, you can't judge a book by its cover, right?

I made a mental note to tell Grandpa Dave my little joke. As you've probably guessed, I didn't have a lot of friends. Not that I wasn't a friendly person. I had a lot of acquaintances. It was just hard for me to get close to people. I wasn't the type to tell my deepest, darkest secrets to someone I hadn't known...well, all my life.

The brawny book man's name was Ford. I'd have been truly delighted had it been Harley, but had you been expecting me to say his name was Fitzgerald or Melville, please see the aforementioned joke about books and covers. He was friendly and invited me to come around and look at his collection anytime. I promised I'd do so after I got settled in.

Then it was downstairs to meet the rest of the shop owners. The first shop on the left when you came in the door--the shop directly across the hall from mine--was Delightful Home. The proprietress was Connie, who preferred a hug over a handshake.

"Aren't you lovely?" Connie asked.

I did not say I doubt it, which was the first thought that popped into my brain, but I did thank her for the compliment. Connie was herself the embodiment of lovely. She had long, honey blonde hair that she wore in a single braid. Large silver hoops adorned her ears, and she had skinny silver bracelets stacked up each arm. She wore an embroidered red tunic that fell to her thighs, black leggings, and Birkenstocks. But the thing that made her truly lovely wasn't so much her looks but the way she appeared to boldly embrace life. I mean, the instant we met, she embraced me. Her shop smelled of cinnamon and something else...sage, maybe.

"Melba, that blue is definitely your color," Connie said. "By the way, did that sinus blend help you?"

"It did!" Mrs. Meacham turned to me. "Connie has the most wonderful products, not the least of which are her essential oils."

I could see that Connie had an assortment of candles, soaps, lotions, oils, and tea blends. I was curious to see what all she did have, but that would have to wait.

"I'm here to help you in any way I possibly can," said Connie, with a warm smile. "Anything you need, just let me know. We're neighbors now."

Mrs. Meacham took me to meet the last of my "neighbors," Mr. and Mrs. Peterman.

"Call us Ella and Frank," Ella insisted. She was petite with salt-and-pepper hair styled in a pixie cut.

Frank was average height, had a slight paunch, a bulbous nose, and bushy brown hair. He didn't say much.

Ella and Frank had a paper shop. They designed their own greeting cards and stationery, and they sold specialty and novelty items that would appeal to their clientele. For instance, they had socks with book patterns, quotes from famous books, and likenesses of authors.

After I'd met everyone, Mrs. Meacham handed me the keys to my shop and went upstairs. Although my shop wouldn't open until the first of September, she'd graciously given me this last week of August to get everything set up.

I unlocked my door and went inside. I was surprised to see Max standing by the window. I started to ask her how she'd got in, but then I saw that there was another door that led to the kitchen. I imagined my space had once been the family dining room. Anyway, it was apparent that the door between my space and the kitchen hallway had been left unlocked. I'd have to be careful to check that in the future.

But, for now, I didn't mind at all that Max was there. Or that it appeared she was wearing the same outfit she'd been wearing yesterday. Must have been some party!

"So, you leased the shop?" Max asked.

"I did!"

"Congratulations! I wish we could have champagne to celebrate."

I laughed. "Me too, but I'm driving."

Max joined in my laughter. "I'm so glad you're going to be here. I think we'll be great friends."

"I hope so." And I truly did. I immediately envisioned Max as my best friend—the two of us going to lunch together, talking about guys and clothes, shopping together. I reined myself in before I got too carried away.

I surveyed the room. The inside wall to my right had a fireplace. I recalled that all the rooms upstairs had them too. But this one had built-in floor-to-ceiling bookshelves on either side of the fireplace.

"Does this fireplace still work?" I asked Max.

"I imagine it would, but it isn't used anymore. The owners put central heat and air in eons ago."

"Just checking. I mean, I wasn't going to light fire to anything. I merely wanted to be sure it was safe to put flammables on these shelves." I could feel my face getting hot. "I'm sorry. That was a stupid thing to say. I'm just so excited—"

"And I'm excited for you. You have nothing to apologize for. How were you supposed to know whether or not the former tenant ever lit the fireplace?"

"You're really nice."

"And you're too hard on yourself. Must you be brilliant and well-spoken all the time?"

"Well...I'm certainly not, but I'd like to be."

"Tell me what you have in store for this place," she said.

I indicated the window. "I'd like to have a table flanked by chairs on either side here." I bit my lip. "Where's the best place around here to buy some reasonably priced furniture that would go with the overall atmosphere of the building?"

"I have no idea. You should ask Connie."

"Connie?" I was actually checking to make sure I'd heard Max correctly, but it so happened that I'd left the door open and Connie was walking by as I spoke.

"Yes?"

"Max was telling me that you might know of a good furniture place nearby," I said.

"Max?" Connie looked about the room. "Who's Max?"

I whirled around, thinking Max had somehow slipped out of the room. But, nope, there she stood...shaking her head...and putting a finger to her lips.

"Um...she was....she was just here. She was here yesterday too. I assumed she was a Shops on Main regular."

"I don't know her, but I'd love to meet her sometime. As for the furniture, I'd try the antique stores downtown for starters. You might fall in love with just the right piece or two there." She grinned. "I'd better get back to minding the store. Good luck with the furniture shopping!"

Connie pulled the door closed behind her as she left, and I was glad. I turned to Max.

"Gee, that was awkward," she said. "I was sure you knew."

"Knew?"

"That I'm a ghost."

Gayle Leeson

Interested in reading more? Designs on Murder, Book One in the Ghostly Fashionista Mystery Series, only 99 cents - www.ghostlyfashionista.com